A
Witchdance in Bavaria

By Noah Webster

A
WITCHDANCE IN
BAVARIA

NOAH WEBSTER

PUBLISHED FOR THE CRIME CLUB BY
DOUBLEDAY & COMPANY, INC.
GARDEN CITY, NEW YORK
1976

All of the characters in this book
are fictitious, and any resemblance
to actual persons, living or dead,
is purely coincidental.

Library of Congress Cataloging in Publication Data
Knox, Bill, 1928–
A witchdance in Bavaria.

I. Title.
PZ4.K748Wi   [PR6061.N6]   823'.9'14
ISBN 0-385-11225-4
Library of Congress Catalog Card Number 75–37818

For Beth and Andy

Queen's and Lord Treasurer's Remembrancer
H. M. Exchequer Office

"Para 30. By the law of Scotland and the Queen's and Lord Treasurer's Remembrancer is entitled *ex officio* to administer without Confirmation (Letters of Administration) or other process of law the assets of companies or estates which fall to the Crown in Scotland."

A
Witchdance in Bavaria

CHAPTER ONE

When it rains in Edinburgh in February it rains in true capital style. Forget the kind of romantic picture-book drizzle that settles gently on the Highlands to the north or even the heavier downpours which make the Lowland golf courses some of the greenest, sweetest playing in the world.

In Edinburgh, the rain in February comes down as whole water from a sullen, lead-grey Scottish sky. It churns along the gutters like a tidal race, it batters the hardiest low-season package tourist into a rush for shelter in a matter of seconds. Left clinging miserably to the rooftops, pigeons keep their wing-feathers closed up tight—and even the great skyline bulk of Edinburgh Castle is washed from sight as if it didn't exist.

Jonathan Gaunt was driving to work when it began raining. To be more exact, he was on his third city-centre cruise along the busy length of George Street, peering through the slapping wiper blades and still hoping for a vacant parking meter. One as near as possible to his destination, because the rain was beating a louder tattoo on the car's roof every moment.

Suddenly, unbelievably, there was an empty space ahead with the car which had left it still driving away. Feeling lucky, Gaunt sent his little black Mini-Cooper sports saloon curving gently towards the precious parking box.

But it was centre parking in George Street and a battleship-sized white Rolls-Royce was nosing towards the same meter from the opposite side, turn indicators the size of spotlamps winking an imperious claim. A fat, equally imperious face showed behind its wheel and hadn't even noticed the little black car.

Instinctively, Gaunt made a fast downward gear change and booted the accelerator hard, in no mood to be thwarted. Surging forward, the Mini-Cooper clawed round into the meter space and braked to a skidding halt before the big chrome status-symbol radiator could get near.

Balked, the fat face in the Rolls-Royce stalled his engine. He shook a fist and mouthed a flow of invective Gaunt hardly needed to lip-read. Then, as horns began sounding behind the stalled car, the fat face reluctantly reversed out and started to drive away.

Grinning, Gaunt gave the man a vigorous V sign in farewell then saw something which completed his victory. The meter had almost an hour's free time left on its dial.

He got out, quickly locked the car, and dived through the downpour to the pavement. A shop overhang gave him shelter for a moment then he was back out in the wet, hurrying in a home run towards the nearby Exchequer Building. By now, the rain was bouncing high off the pavement but he chuckled as he saw a familiar, bulky figure in an equal hurry just ahead.

Lengthening his stride, Gaunt started to catch up. Then he heard a car engine coming close and hard from behind, anticipated the inevitable, and dodged in towards the nearest doorway.

A second later the car roared past only inches from the kerb, wheels throwing the gutter's rain water up and out like a tidal wave. Gaunt escaped, but the bulky figure ahead was drenched from head to foot as the water hit him.

It was the white Rolls-Royce. Swerving out towards the middle of the road again, it drove off, the fat-faced man at the wheel glancing back and scowling his disappointment. Swearing softly, Gaunt loped up to the soaked, forlorn, totally baffled victim, who had come to a sodden, open-mouthed halt.

"Hard luck, Henry," he sympathised cheerfully. "You look like you could use a lifeboat."

Henry Falconer, a big, heavy-faced man and senior administrative assistant to the Queen's and Lord Treasurer's Remembrancer, wasn't easily roused to wrath. But he cursed viciously at the world in general as he joined Gaunt in a final gallop through the rain towards the Exchequer Building. Water still slopping from his clothes, he stopped just inside the lobby and looked down at the damage.

"Damn the idiot," he grated bitterly. "That was deliberate —damned well premeditated. Look at me! I'm soaked to the skin!"

"Some people have a nasty sense of humour," agreed Jonathan Gaunt mildly. "He must have had it in for you, Henry. But never mind—strip off and get your secretary to give you a brisk rubdown. Make her day."

"She's the kind who'd use sandpaper and enjoy it," said Henry Falconer sadly. "Sometimes I think she's in league with my wife." He considered the gradually widening pool at his feet, sighed, then salvaged what remained of his waterlogged dignity. "I'll have to do what I can—I'm due at a meeting with the Remembrancer."

The way he said it made Gaunt raise an eyebrow.

Falconer nodded. "Be in my office in an hour. We've a little job for you, and you'll need your passport."

"Sunshine style?" asked Gaunt hopefully.

"No, snow and cold," said Falconer with a vicious satisfaction. "Pack your winter drawers."

He strode off, water slopping inside his shoes. Gaunt shrugged and headed for his own room. An hour would give him time to check through the day's stock market listings— though with the state of the market that was a penance on its own.

An Exchequer Office secretary, small and blond, tumbled into the lobby through the doorway and stood shaking the rain from her plastic coat.

Gaunt winked at her. She smiled in return, but the rain had made her eye make-up run, and spoiled the effect.

When she found that out later, meeting a mirror, the Exchequer blonde cursed. In the secretarial pool hen-loft Jonathan Gaunt rated a lot of interest. Interest and a puzzle. He was in his early thirties, tall, and with a compact build. He had a likeable, raw-boned face, slightly freckled, moody grey-green eyes, and fair hair which was usually untidy and long by even the most easygoing of modern Civil Service standards.

The hen-loft knew Gaunt was something called an external auditor in the Remembrancer's Office, in itself a strange enough section in the Exchequer Building. But there was something else. He had dated several girls from the hen-loft. He had a reputation for being as healthily normal as any other male around.

But the dating always stayed casual and soon finished, cooled down in friendly style. For some reason, Jonathan Gaunt seemed determined to avoid becoming heavily involved.

She sighed, decided she'd never completely understand men, and started the repair work.

Henry Falconer's office was on the second floor of the Exchequer Building, with a window which looked out on George Street. He'd augmented the government-issue furniture in the big room with a few pieces of his own, including a grandfather clock his wife wouldn't allow him to have at home. But so far he hadn't done anything about the four-by-three patch of regulation green carpet which was the Civil Service entitlement for senior administrative assistant grades.

Four-by-three exactly. Settled behind his desk with the rain still lashing down outside, Falconer scowled at the carpet. Someday he'd get rid of that hated postage stamp of green and—and yes, do something really exotic. Maybe substitute a broad swathe of Andalusian sheepskin and damn the annual inventory consequences.

He sniffed and fought back a sneeze. Already, he was sure

he had a cold coming on and he wondered how long it would take for his clothes to dry in the boiler room. The borrowed golfing sweater and slacks he was wearing were both a couple of sizes too small for him and his socks were still damp.

The grandfather clock in the corner solemnly sounded once, for ten-thirty. The sound brought him back to the papers on his desk and he carefully slid one out of sight, into a drawer. As he closed the drawer, the desk intercom rasped.

Falconer flicked the answer switch.

"Yes?" he asked wearily.

"Mr. Gaunt is here," said his secretary's voice with a cool disapproval. "He says you want to see him."

"That's right. I—uh—forgot to tell you." Falconer felt another sneeze building up and at the same time wondered why he always seemed to be apologising to the woman. "Send him in. Then bring me the rest of the Ritter file."

He just got it out, then the sneeze came. He blew his nose on a tissue, leaned forward to apologise on the intercom, then saw the connection had already been broken and sighed.

Falconer had time to blow his nose again before the door opened. He nodded a brusque greeting as Gaunt came in, and gestured to the chair opposite.

"Thanks." Gaunt sat down, then eyed him with a slight twinkle. "I like the outfit, Henry."

"At least with me it's temporary." Falconer considered Gaunt's clothes with open disapproval. A lightweight grey tweed sports suit with a pink, patterned, button-down collared shirt and broad, dark blue tie, plus slip-on shoes, grated against his own ideas of correct Civil Service wear. "I told you I was meeting the Remembrancer, didn't I?"

"Yes. Did he like the sweater?" asked Gaunt innocently.

Falconer scowled, unamused, and spent a moment sorting through some of the papers on his desk.

"You're going to Munich," he said abruptly. "A debt-collecting mission—about fifty thousand pounds, we believe. So how's your German?"

"I can say *Kamerad*, which is always useful." Gaunt raised both hands in mock surrender, then let them fall again. "No problems. I know enough to get by, and I know Munich."

"Where the current temperature is thirty degrees Farenheit, with snow. The forecast is more snow—I checked," said Falconer with an acid satisfaction. "Today is Friday. We're booking you a flight on Sunday and I'll expect you back here by Wednesday at the latest."

"Thanks," said Gaunt dryly. "All right, Henry, I'm debt-collecting. Who owes who and why?"

"You're going out to talk to a Bavarian named Hans Ritter. He owes us the money—we think." Falconer frowned a little. "To be accurate about it, there's a grey area in our reckoning, one the Remembrancer wants clarified. We've made preliminary contact with Ritter, who hasn't been exactly co-operative. But he's being advised you're coming."

Gaunt shrugged. All kinds of rag-bag problems ended up in the clutch of the Queen's and Lord Treasurer's Remembrancer, pushed that way by other government departments who didn't want to know about them. The antiquated title covered a compact organisation which throughout its entire, long, and deliberately low-profile history had always been around and available.

Across the desk, Henry Falconer took time off to blow his nose again. Gaunt switched his attention to the window and the rain.

Problems—it had always been that way, right from the beginning, when the first, medieval Remembrancer had been a body servant to the early Scottish kings and queens. Then, his task had been to go everywhere with them and remember everything for them—unless he decided it was something they'd rather forget.

Except that gradually the Remembrancer's activities had shifted in emphasis and grown in responsibility, until the mid-1970s brand was a senior-grade professional civil servant who became involved in most things that mattered in Scotland. The department built on other people's cast-offs had become a power in its own right, from being paymaster for every government department north of the border to constituting its own court of law in many a revenue case.

It processed what was vaguely termed "state intelligence." It looked after the security of the Scottish crown jewels, moved in on things like Treasure Trove, got involved with the Ministry of Defence, stuck its nose into the running of the law courts . . . even made sure the civil servants in those other government departments paid the right amount of income tax on their salaries.

And that was only the start of the list.

"Now." Falconer gave his nose a final, trumpeting blow and threw the used tissue into his wastebasket. "I said Hans Ritter knows you're coming, and there's a full briefing in the file. But it comes down to this. Until a year ago a private limited company, Castlegate Custom Building, was registered in Edinburgh with a nominal share capital. From all accounts, it started small and grew fairly quickly—quickly and profitably, with a number of housing projects. There were three directors—Hans Ritter, a John MacIntosh, and Bernard Gorman. They had equal shareholdings but MacIntosh acted as managing director."

"You said 'was registered,'" murmured Gaunt.

Falconer nodded. "Castlegate Building was struck off our official Register of Companies when the directors failed to file the normal annual report of business activities. Companies Branch investigated first, of course. They found the office had been closed, the staff and work-force left without jobs or money—and a number of half-finished houses were scattered up and down the country."

"And our three directors had vanished?"

"Completely." Falconer blew his nose again, noisily. "No one had seen Ritter or Gorman for years. Workmen were dancing up and down about wages due, various creditors wanted paid for supplies, the Inland Revenue began making frantic noises about back taxes they were owed. As managing director, John MacIntosh emptied Castlegate's bank account the day before he vanished."

"An enterprising character," agreed Gaunt dryly, having heard the same kind of story often enough before. "Then we moved in?"

"As usual, *bona vacantia* style." Frowning, Falconer placed a finger on his own wrist and concentrated on checking his pulse-rate against the second hand of his watch.

"Normal?" asked Gaunt as he finished.

"So far but that means nothing." Falconer sighed expansively. "Well, as far as this Castlegate firm was concerned, our role was fairly automatic at that stage."

Gaunt nodded, knowing the drill. Companies Branch of the Remembrancer's Office lived in a private little world of company registers, business names, and partnerships. It performed odd functions like stopping firms using misleading business names or pretending they had royal trading connections. It could—and did—put the boot in hard when it got as much as a sniff of fraud or share-rigging.

But when a company folded up in the way Castlegate had collapsed, Companies Branch stepped in, salvaged any assets remaining, and paid out what it could to creditors. Any time there was cash left over with no claimant, the money "fell to the Crown." Meaning it vanished into the government's coffers.

"How did it end?" he asked.

"Unpaid debts, including back tax, of about twenty thousand." Falconer shrugged. "Not exactly a disaster situation. And if we get this money from Munich—" He stopped there as the door opened and his secretary, a well-built brunette in her thirties, came in.

"You wanted the rest of the Ritter file." She crossed to the desk in a waft of antiseptic perfume, her face as expressionless as chiselled marble, and laid down a brown envelope. Then, beside it, she placed a paper cup of water and two aspirins and pursed her lips, considering Falconer. "You'd better take these. A man your age should know better than go playing in puddles."

"I told you how it was!" protested Falconer. "Now look, Hannah—"

She ignored him and turned, her face still frozen. But Gaunt could have sworn one eye quivered in an amused wink as she passed him and went out again, closing the door.

Sighing, Falconer took the aspirins and washed them down. Then he emptied the envelope on the desk. Out tumbled some sheets of paper, then two surprising items, heavy wristbands made from coloured beads. Absently fingering one of the wristbands, Falconer looked up again.

"I was going to say this money from Munich would square any debts remaining and leave the department with a bonus— which always looks good. How we found out about it is another matter. Castlegate's managing director, John Mac-Intosh, turned up again about ten days ago—dead."

Gaunt looked the way he felt, bewildered. He combed a hand over his untidy fair hair and decided to stay quiet and wait.

"A lawyer in Glasgow contacted Companies Branch," explained Falconer, still toying with the wristband. "He said a client of his named MacIntosh—our MacIntosh, as it turned out—had been killed in an accident. MacIntosh had left personal papers with him, some referred to the Castlegate company, and as he didn't know much about MacIntosh he thought he'd better ask us what to do."

"What kind of an accident?" Gaunt found his cigarettes and lit one.

"Oh, a simple enough thing," said Falconer vaguely. "Mac-Intosh was running a little back-street car-repair business on his own. He was working late one night, something happened, and the place burned down. They found him dead under a car he'd been working on—it looked as if the fuel tank had exploded."

"Nasty." Gaunt drew gently on his cigarette. "How long had the lawyer had the papers?"

"A few months. MacIntosh first used him when he bought the garage. All he knew was that MacIntosh lived alone, didn't seem to have any relatives, and came in now and again to pay the odd bill or sort out some car-trade problems."

"Every car-repair man needs a lawyer," mused Gaunt. "The only people who need one more are his customers."

"Do you listen to me, or do we discuss your views on morality and the motor trade?" asked Falconer bleakly.

"Sorry."

Falconer grunted. "Well, a few days before MacIntosh was killed he happened to call on his lawyer to sort out a business problem. Before he left, MacIntosh gave the man this envelope to keep with his other papers." He tapped the envelope with a stubby forefinger. "All it actually held were these two bracelet things and a note saying they belonged to Ritter—plus Ritter's address in Munich. But that address was what we needed, because in the earlier papers we found an old loan agreement between Ritter and the Castlegate firm."

"Our fifty thousand?" Gaunt whistled as Falconer nodded. "What terms?"

"Unsecured, interest-free, repayable on demand." Falconer's broad face twitched as he fought back the makings of another sneeze. "With luck, I may even survive to see it. Though Ritter claims half the money was paid to buy him out as a director and only half was a direct loan."

"Your grey area." Gaunt stubbed his cigarette on the desk ashtray, which was otherwise empty, then gestured towards the two beaded wristbands. "What about these?"

"Take them with you," shrugged Falconer. "We mentioned them when we wrote and he seems to want them."

Gaunt picked one up. It was handmade, the "beads" actually a mixture of dried seeds and tiny pieces of wood, all carefully threaded together so that their colours formed a pattern, then the whole backed by a tiny strip of faded canvas.

"African?"

"Probably." Falconer retrieved the wristband, dropped both back into the envelope, added the papers, then slid the envelope and the pasteboard file across the desk. "That's everything. You've full authority to make a final agreement."

"All right." Gaunt got up but left the file where it was and walked over to the window and looked out. It was still raining in George Street, but there was a first hint of blue sky beginning to show beyond the rooftops. "Henry, there were three directors. What about the other character, Gorman?"

"He disappeared like MacIntosh, but earlier. Legally, you can forget him." Falconer sneezed this time and swore bitterly into a tissue. "One thing—when you collect, make sure it's a certified cheque and payable in Deutschemarks, not pounds sterling."

"Shame on you," said Gaunt, deadpan. "Henry, that's unpatriotic."

"Not the way exchange rates are wavering," said Falconer defensively. "I'd call it patriotic to be practical."

"All right, Deutschemarks," agreed Gaunt sadly. He came back from the window, stopped by Falconer's grandfather clock, and stood listening to its slow, calm, deep-throated ticking for a moment. "Henry, you'll admit you're low on imagination. But isn't it a hell of a series of coincidences? MacIntosh goes to his lawyer, MacIntosh dies, Ritter's name turns up—"

"I'd call it good fortune, for us." Falconer blew his nose again then thawed his face into a cautious smile. "Ah—before you go, how's the world of stocks and shares treating you?"

Gaunt grinned wryly. Falconer was one of the few people who knew about his stock market hobby interest—and hobby it had to be, on a shoe-string budget that would have been better suited to trading stamps.

"Things are bad," he admitted. "I'm practically a disaster area."

"Difficult times." Falconer hesitated, then plunged on. "But a friend did give me a tip—"

"My tip would be to keep your money in a piggy-bank," said Gaunt firmly. "Piggy-banks are the in thing right now."

"My friend said Trellux Components," said Falconer uncomfortably. "I know how you feel. But—well—"

"I wouldn't know, Henry." The smile died from Gaunt's face as he spoke and for a moment he looked older. It still hurt to be reminded of Patty and their divorce. She'd been remarried almost a year and Eric Garfield, the boss of Trellux Components, a middle-sized company in the computer world, was a man he liked. Someday he'd accept it. But it still—yes, hurt was the word. "Last time I heard from them, it was a Christmas card."

"Of course." Falconer sought refuge in another bout of violent, not completely necessary nose-blowing which ended with an explosively genuine sneeze. He changed the subject quickly. "Well, at least I got the number of that damned Rolls-Royce. There are ways of fixing that kind of driver, once I find out who he is."

"Henry, if you're thinking of asking your pals in Inland Revenue to check him out, I'm surprised." Gaunt shook his head in mock horror. "That's what I'd call downright vindictive, petty, and unethical."

"Yes," said Falconer happily. "You're right. The sooner you leave the sooner I can get it started."

Grinning, Gaunt picked up the manilla envelope and the Ritter file and left.

Once he'd gone, Henry Falconer's expression changed. He blew his nose, gently this time, sighed, then slowly opened the desk drawer and brought out the item he'd kept back from the Ritter papers.

The police report on John MacIntosh's death was terse, formal, and deliberately open-ended. The last curt sentence made that understandable:

"Certain injuries on the deceased's body found during postmortem examination are not wholly compatible with the circumstances in which he met his death, and as a result, though no other evidence to the contrary exists, the case cannot be satisfactorily dismissed as a simple accident."

Falconer chewed his lower lip thoughtfully for a moment, then put the report back in his drawer. He could have told Gaunt, at one point he'd been close to doing just that. But the police could be overcautious and Munich was a long way away.

He stopped there, smiled slightly, and nodded. At the worst, anyway, Gaunt was more than capable of looking after himself.

Falconer lifted the telephone, dialled a number which got him through to the city's Motor Taxation Department, and a minute later was speaking to a suitably sympathetic official about the owner of a certain white Rolls-Royce.

Jonathan Gaunt woke at 7 A.M. on the Sunday, silenced the alarm clock with a bitter thump, and forced his way out of bed a couple of minutes later. Saturday night had ended in a jazz club off Princes Street, a lot later than he had intended, but things had a habit of happening that way.

Shaved and dressed, he countered a low-grade hangover with orange juice and coffee, then wrote a quick note for the cleaning woman who descended on his two-room apartment on Mondays and Wednesdays. He left the note propped against the kettle, where she'd be sure to find it, collected the travel bag he'd packed, and left.

From the apartment to Edinburgh airport took twenty minutes in the Mini-Cooper and the weather was cloudy but dry. He parked the little car, walked over to the terminal building, and checked the bag in at the British Airways desk for the feeder flight to London. Then, as he turned away, a voice hailed him.

"Working, or just plain running away?" The man who stood grinning at him was small, plump, and wore an expensive, hairy sweater over corduroy slacks. "Gaunt, I'm surprised at you. The Sabbath was meant as a day of rest."

"My boss is a professional atheist." Gaunt returned the grin. John Milton, stockbroker, cable address Paradise Lost, Edinburgh, somehow tolerated the small-scale panics and confusions Gaunt threw his way and usually charged minimum commission. He claimed he made up the rest in entertainment value. "What's your excuse?"

"My mother-in-law." Milton sighed at the reminder. "I'm collecting her off the Aberdeen flight—they're probably bringing her down in a cage."

"Hard luck." Gaunt chuckled, then stopped and looked past him.

A new arrival had just marched up to the check-in desk lugging a leather suitcase in one hand and trailing a white raincoat in the other. The man was heavily built, familiarly fat-faced, and wore a dark business suit. There was arrogance in the way he walked and when he talked to the counter clerk his voice reached them as a loud rasp. Turning, Gaunt glanced out towards the parking lot and saw the white Rolls-Royce lying in a space near the exit.

"Know him?" asked Milton with a mild curiosity.

"I've seen him around." Gaunt decided against mentioning the George Street brawl. "Who is he?"

"Harry Green. I'd like to know what he's up to this time." Milton eyed the fat man with a degree of distaste. "He's a fixer, a professional middleman. Sales presentation, a contract blank in his pocket, and a percentage rake-off from both sides when the deal is signed." He shrugged. "The trouble is, he's good at it."

"Who does he work for?"

"Anyone—as long as they're big enough and the money is right," said Milton wryly. "He calls himself an engineer, but what he knows about engineering wouldn't fill an eggcup. His speciality is contacts—and he treats the rest of the world like dirt."

Leaving his suitcase at the check-in desk, the fat man

strode towards the newsstand. He glanced at Gaunt as he passed but gave no sign of recognition and kept on going.

"I'm glad I met you, Jonny," said Milton, bringing out his cigarettes. He gave one to Gaunt and they shared a light. "I wanted to talk to you about something."

"Your mother-in-law?" asked Gaunt dryly.

"Something almost as unpleasant," said Milton sadly. "That rubbish lot of shipping shares you bought last month, the ones you said were due to rise."

"So I was wrong," admitted Gaunt.

"Then get rid of them before they sink," urged Milton. "I mean it."

"I'll think about it." Gaunt drew pensively on his cigarette. The shares had cost four hundred pounds, which he'd hoped to double—and some of that four hundred had been the next quarter's rent money. "Look, I'm going to Munich for a couple of days. I'll call you when I get back."

"No later," warned Milton. "They've a company statement coming out in a week, and it's going to be bad."

"Thanks." Gaunt watched another batch of intending travellers arrive, then, almost reluctantly, asked, "Heard anything about Trellux Components lately?"

The public address system stopped its soft music for a moment and announced the Aberdeen flight had landed.

"Mother-in-law," Milton sighed. "Don't ask me why she just didn't come down on her broomstick. Uh—you said Trellux. Why?"

"I heard them mentioned." Gaunt kept his manner casual.

"I haven't." Milton gave him an old-fashioned look. "But computers are in a healthy scene, so I'm interested. What kind of mention?"

Gaunt shook his head. "Nothing that mattered."

"Well, if it happens again let me know. Unless it's from the same idiot who told you about those shipping shares." Milton stopped and drew a deep breath. "I'd better go—but remember, phone me when you get back."

The chubby stockbroker went off towards the arrival gate.

Gaunt watched him meet a large, elderly woman with a face like weathered granite, then smiled and turned away. Everybody had their problems.

With a strong tail wind, the Trident jet flight to London took an hour. Gaunt had a seat in the mid-section, the aircraft was crammed with passengers, and he didn't see Harry Green.

Once they landed, however, the fat man was just ahead of him in the walk from baggage collection through to the International Terminal. They headed for the same flight desk, Green got there first, and Gaunt winced as he heard him check in for Munich.

There was a flight delay, which meant a couple of hours to spare. Gaunt bought a couple of magazines at a bookstall, then made for the airport bar and ordered a beer. As it arrived, he heard Green's voice snarling somewhere near and turned.

The fat man was at a table, an empty glass in front of him, and was arguing with a waitress about the change she'd brought him. Suddenly, viciously, he pushed back his chair and marched out, leaving the girl white-faced.

Quietly, Gaunt picked up his glass and went over to the girl, who was tidying the table.

"A nasty one," he said sympathetically, nodding towards the door. "Seen him before?"

"No." She mopped the table mechanically. "But I know his kind. He tried to say I was overcharging him."

"I heard." Gaunt looked worried. "Well, if he's a passenger I wouldn't like to be on his plane."

She looked up, puzzled. "Why?"

"I could be wrong." Gaunt hesitated. "But he had an odd kind of bulge under his jacket, near the armpit. Didn't you notice?" He shrugged deprecatingly. "Maybe I've read too many hi-jacking reports—"

"You think it might have been a gun?" She stared at him.

"I don't know," Gaunt said mildly.

"You can't be too careful." A glint came into the girl's eyes. "Well, he's easy enough to spot."

She walked quickly back towards the bar counter and picked up a telephone. Gaunt finished his drink and left.

Half an hour later he saw Green walking towards the immigration counter at international departures and drifted along behind him. They went through and Customs came next with a queue for the inevitable security checks.

As Green approached the barrier two large, uniformed airport police quietly materialised on either side and firmly led him into a corner.

Gaunt went through happily. By then, Green was standing with his hands against a wall, protesting loudly while the two policemen began giving him the full treatment.

Twenty minutes later, when the Munich flight was called, there was still no sign of Green. The aircraft was another Trident jet, but almost half-empty this time, and when the fat man did finally arrive he was the last to board, still flush-faced and angry.

The flight to Munich took an hour and twenty minutes and the cabin staff served an early lunch on the way. By then, the occasional snow-capped Alpine peak had begun showing its tip through the grey cloud far below—and not long afterwards the Trident began easing down with an initial rumble and shudder of hydraulics.

The cloud met them, held them, then wisped away to show an expanse of snow-covered hills and woodland, speckled with tiny villages and a thin tracery of roads. Suddenly, a blanket of falling snow wiped out visibility again and when it died the jet was swinging into its final approach run for Munich airport.

The city below, big and modern with endless rows of high-rise apartment blocks, had gained a few features since Gaunt had seen it last. Some he knew, like the Olympic Games stadium to the north and the needle-like television tower beside it. But there were new factory complexes and a motorway he couldn't remember.

Then they had landed and were taxi-ing in towards the concrete shoe-box terminal building with the snow beginning to fall again. When the Trident stopped, Harry Green was inevitably the first passenger to thrust his way down the gangway steps and into the waiting terminal bus.

Gaunt followed with the others, past a green-clad security guard with a machine pistol who already had snow building on the shoulders of his greatcoat.

Tightening his own coat against the cold, Gaunt decided that for once Henry Falconer had been right in his weather forecasting. But inside the terminal building it was warm, landing formalities were crisply brief, and in under ten minutes he was walking through the Customs barrier with his travel bag in one hand.

Once again, Harry Green's bulky figure was just a few paces ahead. A few people were waiting to meet the arriving passengers, and one of them, a thin-faced, fair-haired man in a brown leather coat, stopped him and said something. Green shook his head and the man shrugged, then tried again as Gaunt came up.

"Herr Gaunt?"

Gaunt nodded.

"Good." The man grinned. "*Bitte*, I was sent by Hans Ritter to meet you. I have a car outside, to take you to him."

"Right now?" Gaunt raised a surprised eyebrow.

"*Ja.* He is waiting." The man reached out a hand. "Let me take your bag, Herr Gaunt."

Gaunt kept his grip on it, frowning. "What's the rush?"

The man shrugged. "*Ich weiss nicht . . .* he just sent me to collect you." He tugged the bag gently. "Okay?"

Gaunt hesitated, the man's face tightened, he gave a fractional nod to someone beyond Gaunt—and things happened quickly.

A figure pushing an empty luggage trolley just beside them suddenly swung it round and lunged it like a battering ram. As the trolley took Gaunt hard in the side and toppled, the travel bag was wrenched from his hand. A woman screamed as the man in the leather coat shoved her aside and began running, clutching the bag to his chest.

Harry Green was just ahead. He swung round, stared open-mouthed, then was knocked sprawling on his back as the man cannoned into him. Green went down, roaring like a wounded elephant, while the man hurdled his thrashing figure and kept on running through the busy concourse area, heading for the exit doors.

Swearing, Gaunt sprinted after him. All around, travellers and airline staff stared, too startled to do anything. A police whistle blew somewhere, but Gaunt had no time for anything but the leather-coated figure ahead.

He closed the gap then, almost at the doors, dived for the man in a skidding tackle which took him just behind the knees. They went down together, slithering along the smooth, polished floor and his quarry gave a yelp of pain as he slammed against a pillar, the travel bag spilling from his grasp and tumbling away.

Scrambling up, the man saw Gaunt coming for him again. One hand dived into a pocket of his leather coat, there was a clack, and a spring-blade knife glinted menacingly. Gaunt stopped, ready to meet the threat, but the thin face showed only fear.

Turning, the man dived out through the doors, barging past a bewildered, elderly couple who were just entering.

Getting past the couple cost Gaunt seconds. Then he was in the open, in time to see the leather coat vanishing aboard a black Volkswagen which was already starting to move. As the passenger door slammed, the car went roaring off through the drizzle of snow.

Another moment, and it had swung in the direction of the

main road, giving him time to notice just one thing before it had gone. The number plate had been carefully obliterated with snow.

Whoever had wanted him met hadn't taken any chances.

Going back into the building, Gaunt picked up his travel bag. There was no sense in looking for the man who'd used the luggage trolley and, further along the concourse, an irate, protesting Harry Green seemed the main centre of attention.

Maybe it would be better if it was left that way, he decided.

A policeman was coming in his direction, struggling through the crowd. Gaunt turned, went back out, and walked along till he found the airport taxi rank.

He boarded the first one, and told the driver to take him into the city.

"*Ja.*" The driver started his engine with a flourish. "*Englander?*"

"Yes." Gaunt couldn't be bothered arguing the point.

"Welcome to Munich," said the man cheerfully, and they started away.

CHAPTER TWO

The snow eased off again during the twenty-minute drive into the centre of Munich, but heavy grey clouds overhead warned it was a temporary reprieve and the steady streams of vehicles on the road kept their headlamps shining. Jonathan Gaunt smoked a cigarette and sat back, trying to make sense out of what had happened at the airport, then eventually gave up and simply watched the streets and shop windows flicker past.

Munich had taken a lot of war damage, but that was a long time ago and the city had made the best of it, laying down a new heritage of broad streets and big, modern buildings that had matured enough to acquire character. His destination, the Peulhoff Hotel, was in that category. A tall, clean-lined tower block, it had a row of bright flags stirring lazily above its doorway as the taxi pulled in.

Paying the driver, Gaunt went into the lobby's air-conditioned warmth and crossed to the busy reception desk. A young clerk with a mid-Atlantic accent and metal-framed spectacles quickly located his reservation and beckoned a porter once he had signed in.

The porter took his bag and led the way across to the elevators. The Peulhoff, Gaunt decided, was higher up the social bracket than the usual reservations made by the Remembrancer's Office. It showed in the furs and diamonds drifting past, the expensive scents in the air, and the quality of the leather brief cases being lugged around by bustling males—those who didn't have an assistant along to do the lugging for them. But whatever the size of the bill, that was Edinburgh's worry.

The thought made him smile as the elevator sighed to a stop on the seventh floor. His room number was 718 and the porter guided him along a carpeted corridor, then opened the door, surrendered the travel bag, and pocketed a tip in one fluid, easy motion.

Gaunt went into the room as the man went off. Closing the door behind him, he dumped the travel bag on a stand and walked past a small bathroom into a large, airy room with broad windows and a king-sized double bed. Then he stopped short, the key still dangling in his hand.

A girl was sitting in a chair by the windows. She stayed where she was, one hand stubbing out a cigarette in an ashtray, and gave a slightly apologetic smile which accepted his surprise.

"Herr Gaunt?" she asked.

"Yes." He glanced at the key, then raised an eyebrow. "I had a feeling they said this was my room."

"Ja." The girl nodded calmly. Slim and of medium height, long, raven-black hair tied back by a white ribbon, she had a fine-boned face with serious brown eyes and an attractively wide mouth. He guessed her age about twenty-five. A leather jacket was lying on the bed and she wore a white wool rollneck sweater with wine-coloured corduroy trousers and short, smartly styled deerskin snowboots. "I told the floor maid you were an old friend and that I wanted to surprise you."

"You did," agreed Gaunt neutrally. He stripped off his coat and tossed it on the bed beside her jacket. "Do I get to hear why?"

"So that I could meet you as soon as you arrived." She got to her feet as she spoke and came towards him. "We had a cable from your office in Scotland telling us when you would arrive. I am Helga Ritter—my brother Hans asked me to be here."

"Did he, now?" Gaunt shoved the room key in his pocket and grinned a little. "Let's see if I can guess the next part. He wants me to go with you right now to where he's waiting."

"Yes." She nodded. "There are reasons—"

"Like there were when someone tried the same thing at the airport?" he asked grimly, cutting her short.

"*Bitte* . . . I don't understand." She stared at him. "You say someone met you at the airport? From Hans?"

"That was the general idea, before he tried to run off with my spare shirts," agreed Gaunt dryly. "Or maybe he was more interested in what else I might be carrying."

"Why?" She looked bewildered.

"I was hoping you could tell me that," he said slowly. "In fact, I'm counting on it. For instance, you still say you're Helga Ritter?"

Silently, she scooped up a leather handbag from beside the chair, opened it, and brought out a plastic-covered pass. Gaunt took it. The pass carried the name Helga Ritter and her photograph and was countersigned and stamped by the Munich airport authority.

"All right, you're Helga Ritter," he agreed wryly, handing it back. "Why the airport pass?"

"I work there, in air-traffic control." She tucked the pass back into her handbag and frowned. "Herr Gaunt, my brother had reasons for not even trying to meet you at the airport. He'll tell you why when he sees you."

"He'd better," said Gaunt shortly. "What were you supposed to do next? Sneak me out by the hotel back door?"

"Yes." She gave a slight, apologetic shrug. "But that doesn't matter now, not when other people know you're here to meet him."

"It might matter to me," said Gaunt pointedly.

"No." Helga Ritter shook her head earnestly. "You aren't involved, believe me."

"If you say so," said Gaunt dryly, remembering the fair-haired man's knife.

That had been involvement enough as far as he was concerned. As a stage-one introduction it had carried its own warning about what might be next on the list.

"Could you forget what has happened and make it to-night?" the girl asked suddenly. "Please. Suppose I met you here at seven—and we used the front door?"

"I might," mused Gaunt. "But I've an old-fashioned notion about liking to know what's really going on."

"I don't know for sure myself," she declared earnestly. For a moment her confidence seemed to waver and she looked strangely helpless. "But Hans is worried, afraid of something —though he tries to hide it. For days now he has been careful about everything he does."

"Does being careful include talking to the police?" asked Gaunt woodenly. "Maybe I had a sheltered childhood, but that's what I'd do."

"*Nein.*" She shook her head quickly. "He says he can't, and I think what happened to you at the airport will make it even more difficult. But—but I meant what I said. You are in no danger, Herr Gaunt."

"I'd like that part in writing," said Gaunt dryly. Then, without being completely certain why, he nodded. "All right, I'll do it. Seven o'clock, like you said."

"Thank you." Helga Ritter looked relieved. Crossing to the bed, she picked up her leather jacket, then walked to the door. As Gaunt opened it, she surprised him with a smile. "You aren't what I expected, Herr Gaunt. I—I'm glad."

Before he could answer she was on her way along the corridor towards the elevators. Rubbing a hand along his chin, Gaunt closed the door and walked over to the windows. His room was at the front of the Peulhoff and looked out across the snow-covered rooftops opposite towards the twin copper domes of the Frauenkirche Cathedral.

He stood there for a moment, the noise of the traffic below filtering up, the red glare of a flashing neon sign across the street reflecting briefly against the glass. The last time he'd been in Munich his mission had been totally different—as one of the hordes of Scottish football fans who had descended on a bewildered Germany to support their team's short-lived participation in the World Cup.

Scotland hadn't made the Munich finals, but Gaunt had had a round-trip ticket and had made the most of it.

He grinned at the memory of a night in a certain Bavarian *Weinstube*, turned away, and unpacked his bag. The file on Hans Ritter and the Castlegate company was at the bottom and he put it carefully on the table by the bed.

They didn't know much about Ritter. In fact, he was little more than a name, the hint that he was aged about forty, and a note that his address in Munich was located in a high-amenity suburb. To which, decided Gaunt, could now be added a high-amenity sister.

Plus the fact that life was getting complicated. Sighing, he kicked off his shoes and lay down on the bed. There was a low, slow, all too familiar aching starting to build in his back. If it got any worse, he had the bottle of pain-killer tablets tucked in beside his shaving kit—but that sliding tackle at the airport had been stupid and one way or another he was going to have to pay for it.

Stretching full-length on the floral bed-cover, he closed his eyes and cursed the ache. When it came, it wasn't much consolation to remember the procession of surgeons who had said he was lucky.

It still wasn't so long ago. Lieutenant J. Gaunt, six years a professional soldier in the Parachute Regiment, had finished that career by spending six months in a military hospital with a broken back after a partial chute failure on a routine training jump. Then, suddenly, he'd become plain civilian Jonathan Gaunt with a token disability pension and a brand-new divorce.

Patty had gone on pretending all the time he'd been in hospital, though he should have guessed. Patty had been young and blond and had married a uniform and a pair of parachute wings. They were just two people for whom it hadn't worked out with no particular blame and at least they'd never had children. A year after the divorce she'd married again and if he'd had to approve anyone he'd have voted for Eric Garfield —not just because he had money.

It had taken him a year, too, a year of drifting with his sole assets a few university terms he'd spent studying law and accountancy before the army. Then, mainly because of his army record being remembered by someone, he'd been offered a job of external auditor with the Remembrancer's Office.

That grey, old-fashioned building had seemed to offer what he thought he needed, a quiet, peaceful routine. Though he'd soon learned differently about both himself and the job. The Remembrancer's Officer had a habit of attracting trouble in all its shades—and Jonathan Gaunt, aged thirty-four and unattached again, had quickly come to realise that he had a lot of living to enjoy ahead.

But not while he had this ache. Getting up, he found the pain-killers and swallowed one. Then he lay down on the bed again, closed his eyes, and slept.

It was dusk outside and snowing again when he woke. His wrist-watch said it was leaving 6 P.M., his back felt pretty near to normal, and the tiredness left from the flight had gone.

Gaunt switched on the bedside radio, punched the selector buttons, and discovered the third was tuned to the American Forces Network programme for Munich. Blessing the North Atlantic Treaty Organisation for that much, he washed, then treated himself to a clean white shirt while the familiar combination of beat music and occasional news headlines filled the room.

When he was finished, he went over to the bedside table and opened the Ritter file. Putting the two beaded wristbands in one pocket, he tucked a copy of the loan agreement form in another, then, after a moment's thought, hid the rest of the file behind a central-heating radiator by the window.

Leaving the room, he walked along the corridor to the elevators, pressed the call button, then glanced at his watch again and decided there was time for a drink in the lobby bar before he had to meet Helga Ritter.

One of the elevator doors opened and he stepped in. Another passenger hurried along the corridor and made it inside before the door closed, and Gaunt stifled a groan. It was Harry Green, and the fat contact man recognised him immediately.

"You." Green glared as the elevator started down. "You're the fellow who was behind me at the airport, the one who nearly had his luggage stolen!"

"That's right," agreed Gaunt cautiously.

"Then why the hell did you disappear like that?" Green scowled at him suspiciously. "The police are still looking for you."

"For me?" Gaunt gave a look of surprised innocence. "Hell —I just decided I didn't want any kind of fuss."

"Well it happened and you left me to cope with it," grumbled Green. "Those damned German *Polizei* kept on asking questions while I stood like a fool not knowing any of the answers." He looked closer at Gaunt, another memory clicking into place. "You came down on the flight from Edinburgh before that, right?"

Gaunt nodded as the elevator doors opened and they stepped out into the lobby.

"I knew I'd seen you before." Green's fat jowels twitched irritably. "What's your name?"

"Gaunt—Jonathan Gaunt."

Green shrugged. "Over on business?"

Gaunt nodded. "I'm a civil servant—I was sent over to see some people."

"Government stuff, eh?" Green's small eyes showed an immediate glint and his manner changed. "Well, let's forget the airport nonsense. Come and I'll buy you a drink. My name's Harry Green—I'm here for a couple of days to clinch a contract deal."

Gaunt followed the fat man as he bulldozed a way through the lobby and into a corner bar. They found a table, Green snapped his fingers at a scantily dressed waitress, and when she brought the two whiskies he'd ordered he paid for them from a thick wad of notes.

"Cheers," said Gaunt vaguely, tasting his drink.

"Luck." Green took a gulp from his glass, then wiped a hand across his lips and considered his guest's compact, muscular frame with a surprising shrewdness. "What's your civil service line, Gaunt? Ministry of Defence?" He winked. "You look like you could be ex-army—sharp-edge style more than the desk-jockey type."

"Exchequer Office," said Gaunt, presenting the half-truth with a show of caution. At the same time, he mentally upgraded the fat man several points and remembered what he'd been told about him. "We get involved with most departments."

"But not income tax, eh?" Green laughed coarsely and bent closer, his voice wheedling. "You Exchequer boys sometimes check government contract deals, right?"

"Sometimes." The bait was there, and the fat man would be satisfied with even a tentative nibble. "I'm pretty new at this game, still finding my way around. It's—uh—good to meet a friendly face."

Green nodded. "Right. And maybe I can show you some of the angles in the contract world, the kind they don't tell you about back home."

For a moment longer Green considered him, then sat back and signalled the waitress to bring another round of drinks.

"On me," he said brusquely, brushing aside Gaunt's murmured protest. "Expenses style—so what the hell?"

Then smoothly, the fat man switched the conversation away to generalities as harmless as the weather in Munich and the state of Scottish football—both of which, in his opinion, were equally bad. But after ten minutes he stopped, glanced at his watch, and shoved his chair back.

"Time I wasn't here." He rose and gave Gaunt a knowing wink. "There's a man I've got to give the full wine and dine treatment before we get together in a committee session to-morrow. But I'll see you around, eh?" He paused, then added, "People like you and I can help each other—it's a fact of life."

Green left, shoving his bulky way through the crowded bar. Sitting back, Gaunt swore softly to himself and revised his assessment a second time. Harry Green was crafty and danger-ous with it, clever enough not to rush anything but obviously already marking him down as a potential addition to his con-tact net.

Except maybe it was time someone played Green at his own game for a spell, then twisted his tail, hard. It was a happy thought, and he picked up his glass again. Harry Green had paid for the drink and somehow that made it taste all the better.

Helga Ritter might have said 7 P.M. but the clock above the lobby of the Peulhoff Hotel read almost half an hour later when she walked in. She stopped, looked around, then smiled as she saw Gaunt coming towards her.

"*Guten Abend* and hello again," he said dryly, reaching her. "I was beginning to wonder if brother Hans had changed his mind." Then he considered her appreciatively. "But I'm glad I waited. The way you look has probably just doubled my credit rating."

She wore a simply cut, scoop-necked dress in green, topped by a white sheepskin coat which she wore loose over her shoulders. Her long black hair, freed from the ribbon, shone under the lobby chandelier as she shook her head and laughed.

"Are women never late in Scotland?" she asked.

"Not if they know what's good for them," declared Gaunt with a mock solemnity. But he meant the rest. Helga Ritter's arrival had registered with just about every adult male around the lobby area.

"Threats?" She raised an equally amused eyebrow, then glanced towards the door. "Well, if you're ready—"

"We'll go," he agreed, taking her arm.

They went out. It was cold in the open, but the snow had stopped and the night sky had cleared, leaving a dusting of stars overhead. The raven-haired girl led the way along a row of parked cars to a white BMW coupe and got in behind the wheel. As Gaunt climbed aboard on the passenger side and closed his door she started the engine—but he stopped her as she reached for the gear lever.

"Two questions first, Helga. Exactly where are we going, and what does your brother do for a living these days?"

She looked surprised. "We live at Harnen, a little place just outside Munich. Half an hour will get us there."

"And Hans?"

"He runs a building company." A touch of bitterness entered her voice. "A prospering company, if that's what you want to know. He—also he has other interests. People like him, and he works hard." Her mouth tightened. "Do you have to sound so much like a debt collector?"

"That's what brought me here," he reminded her flatly. "But that wasn't the only reason why I was asking."

She nodded almost wearily, then flicked the car into gear. The three-litre engine snarled, the clutch engaged with a bite, and they took off in a scream of tyre-rubber which threw Gaunt hard back against the passenger seat. Shooting out into the traffic stream, the white coupe accelerated through a set of lights as they changed to red.

"Are we in some kind of rush?" asked Gaunt mildly as they sped on, overtaking a trundling two-car tram.

"No." Her eyes checked the rear mirror, then the rev counter bounced as she changed gear and almost tail-slid the car round a corner. "I want to be sure of something."

"Like we're not being followed?" he sighed, understood,

and hoped the local traffic police had taken their radar meters home for the night.

Heading west, they quickly left the heart of the city behind. Gradually the girl relaxed a little and their pace eased as they skirted the snow-covered gardens of the Nymphenburg Park. Gaunt had a glimpse of boarded-up fountains and turreted silhouettes before they were lost behind the curtain of slush being thrown up by the tyres.

Signposted as leading to the Stuttgart autobahn, the road stayed busy till they left it to join a minor route. Two kilometres on, the car turned off again, this time on an even narrower road which was covered in rutted snow and snaked up a tree-covered hillside.

At the top of the rise, they emerged at the start of a cluster of small, modern houses. Down below, beyond the trees, Munich showed as a vast glow of light which filled most of the horizon.

"This is Harnen," said Helga, slowing the car. She smiled at him in the glow of the dashboard lights. "It's quiet up here —but Hans and I like it that way and we're still close to the city."

The car turned down a lane, bounced along the rough surface for a minute, then its headlamps showed another house ahead. It was older than the others they'd passed, with a high-pitched roof and ornate wooden shutters, and two cars were already parked outside the door.

They stopped beside the other cars, got out, and walked along a narrow path cleared through the snow. As they reached the house the door opened and a man frowned out. He was small and powerfully built, wore a dark wool shirt with heavy grey serge trousers, and looked in his early thirties.

"Helga?" he made her name a low-voiced question.

"*Ja* . . . everything was fine, Karl," she said cheerfully. "So don't keep Herr Gaunt out in the cold."

The man grunted and stood back to let them enter. Then he carefully closed and locked the door again. Gaunt took off his coat and let the small man hang it on a hook beside a Mauser hunting rifle.

"This is Karl Strobel, my cousin," explained Helga. "He works with Hans."

The two men exchanged nods, then she led the way along the hallway into a big, comfortably furnished room which had a log fire burning and crackling in a rustic brick hearth. A tall, thin man standing near the fire came forward, a faint smile on his lips.

"My brother, Hans," said Helga simply.

"Thank you for coming, Herr Gaunt." Hans Ritter gave a fractional bow, then held out a hand from which the ring and little finger were missing. His grip was still firm and friendly. "You've been patient, remarkably patient." The smile twisted a little. "In fact, I'm in your debt in more than one way now."

"I came because I was curious," said Gaunt neutrally. "Your sister also promised I'd get some answers."

Ritter nodded. If he was around forty, he looked older. A lean face and prematurely grey hair made it hard to be sure and he had sharp but heavily lidded eyes which gave the impression they would miss little. At the same time he seemed prosperous enough. His dark blue business suit had been custom-tailored and he wore a white, beautifully cut shirt with a dark red tie.

"When my sister makes a promise I usually try to keep it," said Ritter. He glanced at Helga. "Where's Karl?"

"Probably in the kitchen, with Anna." She tossed her sheepskin coat carelessly over a chair. "I'll go through and see them in a moment."

"Karl and his wife live with us," explained Ritter. "Helga and I are kept busy in our own ways, which makes it a good arrangement. And the house is big enough." Then he paused and brightened. "Helga, if you drove in your usual way then our guest deserves a drink. Whisky, I imagine—in Scotland, it seemed to me that even the babies preferred it to milk."

"Whisky will do," agreed Gaunt absently as the girl went over to a table set with glasses and bottles.

His attention had switched to a small square of blue velvet on the wall opposite the fireplace. The velvet acted as a backcloth to a heavy, multi-layered collar of beads which had to be African work. Instinctively, he patted a hand against the pocket which held the two wristbands and took a step closer.

The collar, which would have stretched from the wearer's throat to cover most of the upper part of the chest, had been threaded and woven into an intricate pattern of colours. Hundreds of beads had been used, from some which were large and wooden and the size of walnuts to others which were mere tiny droplets of coloured glass. Their colours glinted in the bright, flickering light of the burning logs.

"Yabanzan tribal work, Herr Gaunt." Ritter was at his elbow. "The real thing—a witchdoctor's ceremonial necklace. In fact, a very important witchdoctor's necklace. The beading arrangement tells that." He gave a faint chuckle. "Out in the villages, at least, any African who saw a man wearing it would still dive for cover."

"You got it out there?" asked Gaunt.

"No. A friend sent it—as a gift." Ritter paused as his sister brought over three glasses on a tray. He took his own and raised it in a stoney toast. "Isn't there a Scottish saying about people who borrow money? Something about debtors and lenders?"

"Yes." Gaunt tasted the whisky, a quality single-malt, and eyed the thin, grey-haired man thoughtfully. "It goes 'neither a debtor nor a lender be'—the man who thought it up reckoned there was trouble waiting either way."

"A wise man, indeed." Ritter twisted a wry smile. "But on that subject, the letter from your Remembrancer said John MacIntosh had left something for me—something you would bring out with you."

Gaunt nodded, produced the two beaded wristbands from his pocket, and quietly laid them on the palm of Ritter's outstretched, mutilated hand.

"*Danke.*" Ritter quietly turned away and examined the wristbands for a moment under the bright light of a table lamp. Then, his face empty of expression, he laid the wristbands on the table.

"Are they what you expected?" Helga joined him, looked at the wristbands, and appeared puzzled.

"Yes. I told you about them once—a long time ago. Remember?" Ritter paused, then eyed her cautiously. "Helga, you wanted to see Anna. Why not do that? Herr Gaunt and I need a few minutes alone."

"I think I should stay," she said with an immediate, stubborn frown.

"Why?" Ritter smiled at her. "You already know all I'm going to tell him."

"Do I?" The girl looked ready to argue. Then she sighed, gave a reluctant shrug, and went out, closing the door behind her.

Still smiling, Ritter gestured Gaunt towards a chair beside the fireplace. He took another opposite, as Gaunt settled back, the tall, thin Bavarian considered him carefully for a moment.

"These questions you want to ask," he said slowly. "Let me guess them. You want to know why someone who called you by name tried to steal your baggage at the airport. You want to know why my sister acted so—well, so strangely at your hotel. Correct?"

"For a start," said Gaunt evenly. Trying to gauge Ritter was difficult. He already found him likeable, but there was something else about the man, a hint of underlying tension. "I reckon it's time I knew what was going on."

"Suppose I say it is none of your business?" countered Ritter. He leaned forward, thin fingers clasped together. "You came to Munich with a task. My advice is that you complete that task, then leave."

"Otherwise, I could get hurt?" queried Gaunt.

Ritter chewed his lips. "I didn't say that. But—perhaps."

"Without even knowing why?" asked Gaunt dryly. "Sorry, you'll need to try harder. Like why you don't want the police involved."

"I decide my own priorities," said Ritter quietly. "Last month I was invited to stand for election to the *Landtag*, our state legislature. If I am elected, then other things have been suggested—possibilities too important to jeopardise in any way."

"You mean you're worried about what the police might dig up," said Gaunt bluntly, watching the man closely.

"*Warum nicht* . . . why not?" Ritter switched his gaze towards the fire, his hooded eyes suddenly tired slits. "Like every man, I have a few secrets best left forgotten." He paused and seemed to make up his mind. "All right, perhaps you are due some explanation. Maybe even a little more than Helga knows. Because if you ever thought to repeat it—well, you are a stranger here, you could have your own problems with the police. Anyway, I would simply call you a demented liar."

"You'll make a good politician," mused Gaunt, twisting a grin. "You've got the knack. Go on."

Ritter shrugged. "I'm not ashamed of the things I'm talking about. But if they became public—well, my political opponents would find it easy to twist them enough to stop me being elected."

"So we're talking about blackmail?"

Ritter shook his head and didn't answer, still staring at the fire.

"Then what the hell else?" demanded Gaunt with an impatience he immediately regretted. "Look, Ritter, right now you're practically a government investment, part of keeping the British pound afloat in your own small way. I could say that makes trying to help you almost part of my job."

"Till I pay?" For a moment, Ritter found a wisp of amusement in the idea, then he shook his head again. "There's Helga."

"Helga is your problem," declared Gaunt. "She won't hear anything from me."

Still fighting indecision, Ritter used a poker to stir fresh, crackling life from the burning logs. Then, slowly, he put the poker down.

"I don't understand it completely myself," he said simply. "It comes from the past. I think I can deal with it, but there is an outside chance—a ridiculous chance—that someone may try to kill me."

"Since when was there anything ridiculous about being killed?" Gaunt stared at him.

Ritter sucked his teeth. "This time there is. Herr Gaunt, for several days now I have had the feeling that I have been followed—that this house was being watched. Then my office was broken into during the night but nothing taken." He shrugged. "At first, I wondered if it was political—we have extremists like every other country and I have taken a very public stand against them. But I know better now."

"Why?" asked Gaunt, puzzled.

"Three reasons," said Ritter bluntly. "First, the letter from your Remembrancer about John MacIntosh's death started me wondering. Then there was what happened to you at the airport. But the most important reason—well, you brought me that tonight."

Suddenly, Gaunt understood. He got to his feet and went to the table where the beaded wristbands lay.

"These?"

Ritter nodded. "When John MacIntosh arranged things so that both these wristbands would come to me he—ach, he must have feared he was going to die. If it happened, this was his way of warning me."

"He died in a fire," said Gaunt softly. "It was an accident."

"Of course." Ritter shrugged politely.

"Are you trying to tell me that he might have been killed because of these things?" asked Gaunt, frowning at the wristbands.

"*Nein.*" Ritter got up and came to join him. "Tell me, do these look alike to you?"

"Near enough," agreed Gaunt.

"But not exactly. One was his, this one is mine." Ritter lifted the nearest of the cotton-backed bands and slipped it on his wrist. "This was all the security John MacIntosh needed when I arranged my loan—because to us they had their own value, like a medal." A faint, grim smile creased the corners of his mouth. "That was why they were made, Herr Gaunt."

"In Africa?"

Ritter nodded, then went over to the bottles and poured himself a second drink.

"Suppose you're right and MacIntosh was killed," persisted Gaunt. "Wouldn't that make it even more sense for you to get help? You couldn't vote in the *Landtag* if you were dead."

"I know politicians who would challenge that view," said Ritter wryly. He took a swallow from his glass. "I'm not as big a fool as I sound. Before I do anything I want to be sure—I have to be sure when it could cost so much. Then—well, perhaps John did die in an accident. There is such a thing as coincidence."

"But suppose you're right?"

"Nothing would happen to me straightaway." Ritter sounded positive. "These people want something—something I haven't got, whatever they may think. If I have a chance to talk to them, I think I can make them see sense. In fact, now I know more for sure, I feel a lot easier."

"And it all goes back to Africa?"

Ritter nodded.

"Then you know who is on the other end of this?" asked Gaunt sharply.

"That's the impossible part," said Ritter softly. "I should— but I don't." He drew a deep breath. "That's all I want to say for now, Herr Gaunt. Perhaps I've already said too much. But I'm trusting you."

Gaunt saw the man's rock-hard determination and gave a reluctant nod. "If that's how you want it."

"It is." Ritter showed relief, then, with a glance at his watch, changed his mood. "That leaves the real business which brought you here. But—well, Helga thought you might eat with us tonight. If you like the idea, we could leave the Castlegate debt business until tomorrow."

"That suits me—and thanks," said Gaunt, feeling he already had enough on his mind. "Where will we meet?"

"At my office, in the morning. Though I should give you fair warning," said Ritter half-humorously. "Your people may say I owe fifty thousand pounds. I hold proof that the amount is only half that figure. But we can go into that to-morrow, eh?"

"I'm always ready to listen," said Gaunt neutrally.

"Good." Ritter eased the beaded wristband farther up his wrist until it was almost hidden by his shirt cuff. "By then, I may even have other news for you."

"Castlegate Building had three directors," mused Gaunt. "You and MacIntosh and somebody called Bernard Gorman. Did Gorman have a wristband?"

"*Ja.* But he died in a plane crash in South Africa two years ago." Ritter reached for the door handle, then stopped for a moment. "Only five of these wristbands were made, one for each of five men. As far as I know, I should be the only one still alive."

Then he opened the door and waved Gaunt through.

It was a good meal, plain cooking in the lavish Bavarian style, and it was served at a big oak table in a vast kitchen which, despite its old-fashioned air, incorporated a full range of domestic appliances. Gaunt sat next to Helga, with Karl Strobel and his wife across from them. Anna Strobel was a plump, fair-haired girl in her twenties who bustled nervously between courses, helping Helga and trying hard to avoid Gaunt's gaze.

Another time and he might have enjoyed the meal. But it was ruined by the uneasy tension which hung in the air. In fact, the only outwardly relaxed individual was Hans Ritter.

Joking one moment, telling a story from his time in Scotland, or explaining his preference for the dark, richly spiced Wurttemberg wine he poured, Ritter worked hard at trying to ease the mood of the others. He had some small success with Helga, but Strobel and Anna continued to look unhappy.

At last, as Helga brought coffee, Ritter gave a groan of despair and slapped the table with the flat of his good hand.

"I've seen livelier wakes than this," he declared indignantly. "Karl, cheer up—you, too, Anna."

"Have we anything to be cheerful about?" asked Strobel wearily, ignoring a warning nudge from his wife. "Hans, you're the one who told us to be on our guard. If we even knew what was likely to happen—"

"I know," soothed Ritter. "You've been patient, Karl. But things are clearer now—I'd even say better, thanks to our guest. With luck, it will be settled and we can forget about it by this time tomorrow. I mean that."

"Is that true, Herr Gaunt?" Anna Strobel waited anxiously, moistening her lips.

"Well"—Gaunt hesitated, then felt Ritter's foot nudge him under the table—"yes, it could be."

The girl gave a sigh of relief, though her husband still didn't look convinced.

"Tomorrow," promised Ritter cheerfully. "You'll see." A new thought struck him and he turned to Gaunt. "If we've got to talk about problems, there's one difficulty about our own business and tomorrow. We can meet as arranged. But even if we agree, settlement will have to wait a couple of days. Isn't that right, Helga?"

Helga had been standing in the background, listening but saying nothing. She nodded.

"This is *Fasching* time," explained Ritter. He saw Gaunt's total lack of reaction and appealed to his sister. "You tell him what I mean, Helga."

"*Fasching* is our annual carnival time." Helga glanced at the other girl and they exchanged a small, private smile. "For two days everything stops—stops everywhere, even in the villages—and *Fasching* takes over."

"Then, at midnight on Tuesday, it ends again," added Anna with a surprising enthusiasm. "On the Wednesday—"

"It is Ash Wednesday, when we repent and recover," said Ritter dryly. "Eh, Karl?"

Strobel gave a sheepish, unexpected grin.

"Karl met Anna at *Fasching* time two years ago," said Helga, a new twinkle in her eyes.

"And he has been repenting every since," said Ritter solemnly. "Anyway, what matters is I can't make banking arrangements until the holiday is over." He stopped, then brightened and slapped the table again. "The answer is simple. Jonathan, we are going to stop being formal. You'll be our *Fasching* guest. *Ja* . . . I insist."

Gaunt glanced warily towards Helga. She looked surprised and uncertain.

"Hans—" she began.

"Why not?" demanded Ritter. "Karl and Anna have their own arrangements, but we can look after Jonathan. Anyway, *Fasching* is no time for a stranger to be left alone—and with that luck I talked about we may have special reason to celebrate, eh?"

She nodded with a faint trace of reluctance. Gaunt's agreement seemed to be taken for granted—and at least the atmosphere in the room had thawed. Ritter produced another bottle of Wurttemberg and for a spell the conversation flowed more easily. Then, at last, Ritter gestured towards an antique farmhouse clock on the wall.

"Jonathan, you've had a long day," he declared. "It's time

we got you back to your hotel. Karl, will you take my car and drive him in?"

Strobel nodded. In the general movement that followed, Gaunt found himself left alone for a moment with Helga.

"I'd drive you back," she said almost apologetically. "But I've an early start tomorrow—I'm on duty at the airport at 6 A.M."

"My hard luck." He smiled at her. "You could have given me some tips about pitfalls at *Fasching* time."

"And you could have told me if what Hans said tonight was really true," she said quietly. "Was he just putting on an act—or are things really better?"

"He seems to reckon he can cope," answered Gaunt cautiously. "I wouldn't know."

She shook her head doubtfully, but before she could say more Ritter and Strobel returned, bringing his coat. Gaunt pulled it on, said good night, and went out of the house with the two men.

It was a clear, moonlit, bitterly frosty night and Ritter's car, a black Mercedes-Benz, had a thin, fresh crust of frosted snow over its roof and windows. Reaching it first, Strobel opened the driver's door, then drew back with a grunt of surprise.

Pushing past him, Ritter swore softly and lifted a small, doll-shaped figure made from straw from the driver's seat. He looked at it grimly for a moment, then turned to Gaunt.

"A little messenger," he said in a grating voice. "A devil doll." The remaining fingers of his mutilated hand shifted to the doll's throat and tightened. "In Yabanza it is sent as a warning."

"What kind of warning?" asked Gaunt grimly.

"To stay silent and expect a visitor." Ritter gave a grunt of satisfaction. "I was right. But there is a ritual to complete, in case we have an audience."

He turned and murmured a question to Strobel, who fumbled in his pockets and handed over a box of matches.

Still holding the doll, Ritter struck a match, shielded its tiny flame for a moment, then applied it to the straw of the devil doll. The straw flared, and he held the little figure while the flames ate up its length. At the last moment, he tossed the last small portion into the night, where it glowed, then died as it melted the snow.

"Now they know I understand," said Ritter softly. "A child's trick, to try to frighten me. But this time, it works the other way round."

He slapped Gaunt on the back, then nodded to Strobel, who got into the car and started the engine. Gaunt went round to the other side and got aboard. As they drove off, the tall, thin figure waved once, then strode back into the little, high-roofed house.

It was midnight when the car reached the Peulhoff Hotel and along the way Karl Strobel avoided conversation. When Gaunt got out and thanked him, Strobel's answer was a grunt and a nod, then the car pulled away again, heading back towards Harnen.

The hotel lobby was quiet as he collected his key from the night desk and Gaunt was the only passenger in the elevator up to the seventh floor. But as he got out he heard singing and loud laughter and saw a foursome in evening dress wandering their way along the corridor.

A door suddenly flew open, the gross, pyjama-clad figure of Harry Green glared out at the revellers, and his voice snarled complainingly. Then the door banged shut again. Startled, the foursome stood for a moment muttering among themselves before going on their way.

Gaunt followed them along the corridor until he reached Green's door. A breakfast card hung from the handle, signed and ticked for the morning. Green wanted fruit juice, English tea, and a portion of bacon and eggs.

Yielding to schoolboy temptation, Gaunt took out his pen and carefully ticked another half-dozen items from hot chocolate to smoked eel and a double portion of stewed prunes. Then, leaving the breakfast card swinging, he went to his own room.

Going in, he closed the door and glanced around. The bed had been turned down and there were fresh towels in the bathroom. Crossing to the radiator, he retrieved the Ritter file from its hiding place and opened it, flicking through the papers.

His lips shaped a silent whistle. Everything was still there, but in a slightly different order from before. Laying down the file, he quietly checked the drawers in the room. Again, nothing was missing. But the few items in them had also been disturbed in small ways as if the searcher had tried to be careful but had been pressed for time.

That left another possibility. Slowly and thoroughly he began a new, systematic search of the room and found what he had expected when he came to the underside of the dressing table.

The radio transmitter bug was not much bigger than a pack of cigarettes, lightweight, and held in place by tape. But he knew the type. It could eavesdrop and broadcast to a receiver which might be located anything up to half a mile away.

Gently, Gaunt loosened the tape and laid the bug on the bed. He undressed, washed, then collected the bug again and took it into the bathroom.

"*Gute Nacht*," he said cheerfully to whoever was at the other end. "Pleasant dreams."

Then he flushed the bug down the gleaming white toilet bowl, switched off the light, and climbed into bed.

CHAPTER THREE

Jonathan Gaunt woke with edges of bright sunlight streaming in around the window curtains and a vague feeling that some-one not far away was having a try at starting World War III.

Hazily, he glanced at his wrist-watch and saw it was 8 A.M. The noise, a muffled, angry shouting, continued. Then, as he properly wakened, he recognised Harry Green's voice doing the shouting. From the sound of things, the fat man had just received breakfast and wasn't amused. The noise died down, and Gaunt hauled himself out of bed, padded over to the door, and opened it a crack.

He was in time to see Green's room door open and a waiter emerge, dragging a laden trolley. As the waiter shoved the trolley sadly along the corridor towards him, Gaunt opened the door wider and signalled the man. Going back to his clothes, he got a twenty-mark note, returned, and handed it over with a wink.

The waiter's mouth creased in an understanding smile and he went off, whistling as he pushed the trolley.

Washed and shaved, Gaunt ordered breakfast by tele-phone, then dressed while he listened to the tail-end of an A.F.N. news broadcast. The world seemed in its usual mess and he switched off in disgust after a couple of minutes.

The same waiter brought his order of coffee, rolls, and Ba-varian *Sauerkirsch* cherry juice and departed with a conspir-atorial grin. Gaunt ate, found there was enough coffee left in the pot for another cup, and had just poured it when there was a knock on the room door.

Lighting a cigarette, he ambled over and opened it.

"Herr Gaunt?" The man in the corridor was medium height and stocky, with a bright red rose in the buttonhole of his dark blue suit.

"That's right." Gaunt raised a questioning eyebrow.

"*Kriminalinspektor* Dieter Mayr, Munich police." His visitor flicked a warrant card briefly and it vanished again. Bald, with a fringe of short, mousey hair, he looked about forty and had a pock-marked face that might have been weathered from rough, yellowed rock. "*Bitte,* I would like a word with you."

"Come in then." Gaunt waited till the man had walked past him into the room, then closed the door and followed him cautiously. "What's your problem, Inspector?"

"You, Herr Gaunt." Watery blue eyes glanced briefly at the breakfast table. "I came early so we could meet before you might—ah—leave for the day."

"At home, our cops call it catching the early worm." Gaunt gestured towards a chair and, as the man sat down, returned to his own chair beside the breakfast tray. "Well, what kind of problem am I supposed to be?"

His visitor's shoulders twitched a shrug. "You arrived in Munich yesterday, by air from London. Correct?"

Gaunt nodded.

"At the airport, you had a scuffle with a man who tried to steal your luggage." A scowl crossed the yellowed face. "Then you left almost as quickly as the thief, Herr Gaunt. It has taken some time and trouble to trace you. Why didn't you wait?"

"Nothing was stolen, nobody was hurt." Gaunt drank from his coffee cup and kept his expression mildly neutral. "I didn't want to make any kind of fuss."

"One of your fellow-passengers did." Mayr's scowl stayed in place. "Your passport, please."

Gaunt got up, found the passport, and brought it over. After flicking through the pages for a moment, Mayr considered him again with a slightly puzzled frown.

"So, you are a British civil servant. Are you here officially or as a tourist?"

"Officially," said Gaunt. "I've got a job to do that will take a couple of days."

Mayr's lips pursed thoughtfully. "Then one of our government departments can vouch for you, *nicht wahr?*"

"Sorry." Gaunt shook his head sadly. "I'm here to settle an arrangement with one of your local businessmen."

"His name?"

"Hans Ritter," answered Gaunt easily. "He's some kind of local politician."

Mayr nodded briefly. "And your business with him?"

"Strictly private and strictly legal," said Gaunt bluntly. "Inspector, if you want to check me out the easy way, try the British Consulate."

He sounded more confident than he felt, knowing that the British Consulate would probably have met the inquiry with a blank-eyed stare. Admitting to owning a wandering civil servant was something which a prudent consulate would pass along to embassy level.

"Most people in Munich know Herr Ritter." Bleakly, Mayr fished a long, thin cheroot from his top pocket, bit off the end, then used the rest like a pointer. "This man at the airport—how would you describe him?"

"Thin and rat-faced," said Gaunt warily. "He had fair hair and a leather coat."

"And the second man, the one with the luggage trolley?"

Gaunt shrugged. "I knew he was there, that's all."

"*Danke,*" said his visitor with a weary sarcasm. "Anything else you remember or know that might help, Herr Gaunt?"

Tempted, Gaunt hesitated, then slowly shook his head. "No."

"A pity." Mayr used a match to light his cheroot and drew on it with a gloomy air. "Little thieves are always the worst, and Munich at *Fasching* time draws some of them like a magnet. Then we have tourists, the military, foreign workers—all stirred into the third largest city in West Germany."

"So you won't get your luggage thief," paraphrased Gaunt.

"We found you," reminded Mayr dryly. He used a fingertip

to shift a fragment of cigar ash which had landed on the flower in his lapel. "This is Rose Monday, Herr Gaunt. Only fools and the *Polizei* do any work today. Even your British Consulate is closed." He hauled himself to his feet. "Will you be staying on at this hotel?"

Gaunt nodded.

"Good." The yellowed face twisted a humorless grin. "Then I may see you again." Turning on his heel, he strode to the door, opened it, and glanced back. "Enjoy *Fasching* time."

He left, and the door closed hard behind him. Gaunt sighed, tried the coffee again, and found it was cold. Not that it mattered—he sat where he was and called himself a fool. The chance had been there to unload the whole Ritter business and let someone else worry about it, someone who was paid for that kind of worry.

Except that he'd promised Ritter to stay quiet. The kind of fool promise he should never have given.

Back in Edinburgh, the Ritter assignment had seemed easy and reasonably straightforward. Fly out, fly back, buy some duty-free bottles on the plane.

But he should have known better. Gloomily, Gaunt looked out of the window. The snow on the rooftops across the street had started to melt in the sunlight. The same sunlight was throwing his reflection on the window glass, and he considered it wryly.

All politicians went soft in the head when ambition beckoned. That went double for the ones like Ritter, who wanted to go off on their own private crusades and who didn't know there was a thing called the system waiting to process them to standard size.

Helga Ritter would be at work at the airport. He thought of calling her, demanding that she get her brother to see sense. Except that she'd probably tried long and hard already.

Still thinking of the girl, he grinned a little at his own reflection. Given the chance, he'd like to get to know her a lot better. But then, dark-haired girls were the ones who usually attracted him now.

Because Patty was a blond? The grin became a lop-sided twist as he tried to imagine what a psychiatrist would have made of that one. Or done about it.

He rose, stretched experimentally, and decided his back felt reasonably good again. But a short spell at one of the isometric exercises they'd taught him before he left hospital might make sense.

When a plump, flaxen-haired chambermaid walked in a little later, Jonathan Gaunt was hanging by his fingertips from the top of the bathroom door. The girl showed no surprise, murmured a greeting, and left again with the breakfast tray.

That, Gaunt decided, was the sign of a good hotel.

Overnight, the lobby of the Peulhoff had acquired a new, suppressed, but positive atmosphere, as if a slow-burn fuse had been lit and everyone knew what was waiting at the end of it.

When Gaunt emerged from an elevator he found the desk clerk and most of the lobby staff had rosebuds pinned to their lapels. The same went for many of the guests around, including a cluster of new arrivals who were checking in and had airline tags on their baggage.

He eased past their excited chatter, cornered the hall porter, and got the name of a car-rental firm from him. Then he turned to go, and almost collided with the bulky figure of Harry Green.

"Gaunt!" The fat man's face switched an immediate, made-to-measure smile. "I wanted to see you. Ah—got your police problem sorted out?"

"I've talked to them." Gaunt left it at that.

"If they become annoying, let me know. I've a friend who can murmur where it matters." Green glanced at the lobby clock, where the hands were coming up for 9 A.M. "I'm being collected in a minute, then I've a business meeting that will last the morning. But how about lunch here, around twelve-thirty?" He gave a sly wink. "I've still a feeling you and I could be useful to each other."

"Fine." Gaunt looked suitably grateful. "You said a business meeting—I thought the whole town was on holiday?"

"Not the people who matter." Green took a glance around, then added in a softer voice, "I'm in a deal where everybody is moving fast. But Harry Green always moves that little bit faster."

"That's no surprise," murmured Gaunt dutifully. "I'm looking forward to our talk."

He left Green and headed for the main exit and was almost there when a hand grabbed his arm.

"What the hell are you doing in Munich, Jonny boy?" demanded a surprised, delighted voice.

He swung round in disbelief, then grinned at the man in an American major's uniform who had stopped him.

"I thought they'd have court-martialled you by now," declared Gaunt. "Since when did you rate major?"

Bill O'Brien had been a U. S. Air Force lieutenant when they'd last met. That had been at the tail-end of a particularly hairy series of Anglo-American night manoeuvres when, leading their respective sections, they'd met head-on halfway up a mountain in Norway. American and British had immediately claimed to have wiped out the other—then settled it by deciding that if they were both officially dead they might as well go out and get drunk together.

"The great American people finally realised my true worth," said O'Brien, deadpan, as the greetings ended. Then his manner changed. "I—uh—heard what happened in that last drop of yours, Jonny. Thought of writing a couple of times—but what do you say?"

"I could have sold you my jump boots at bargain price," said Gaunt cheerfully. "Forget it. I'm a God-fearing civil servant now. What about you?"

"I'm the original desk-bound warrior—they dumped me into Supply and Administration, based in Munich," admitted O'Brien sadly. Then his eyes took on a cautious glint. "Jonny, how well do you know that fat character you were talking to back there?"

"Green?" Gaunt sensed more than idle curiosity behind the question. "We came out on a plane together, that's all. Now he wants to buy me lunch. Why?"

"He's worth watching," frowned O'Brien. "I'm the office boy for a NATO military purchasing committee in session out here. They—well, they're in the final stage of placing some king-sized contracts for new installations."

"And Green?" prompted Gaunt.

"We're buying, he's selling," said O'Brien cryptically. "Green is in there pitching some hefty sales talk, and there are only two companies left in the running. Computers, Jonny—the way they talk, they don't need soldiers any more. Just computers and a supply of white coats."

"Computers," said Gaunt slowly and thoughtfully. "Who does Green sell for?"

"An outfit called Viped International." O'Brien grinned and lowered his voice. "The rest is confidential, but I'll tell you anyway. We've narrowed down to a couple of British firms, Viped and a smaller outfit called Trellux." He paused, puzzled by Gaunt's reaction. "Something wrong?"

"No," said Gaunt. But Trellux meant Eric Garfield and Patty and a momentary wince. He forced a quick smile. "Bill, I'm only in Munich for a couple of days but we'll have to get together."

"How about tonight?" suggested O'Brien enthusiastically. "This town is scheduled to go crazy, believe me."

"I'm tied up." Gaunt shook his head.

"Tomorrow, then," said O'Brien positively. "I'll fix the details, then get to you. But if you want to contact me in between, they know me here so you'll find Supply and Admin.

in the book." He looked past Gaunt, gave him a quick, fare-well slap on the shoulder, then hurried off to intercept an army colonel who had just emerged from an elevator.

Despite the snow and slush, there was a hint of spring in the air outside the Peulhoff Hotel—spring mixed with car-nival. A group of students went frolicking past, all dressed as pirates. A uniformed cop on crossing duty watched them in-dulgently, a sprig of greenery stuck in his pistol holster, while some of the taxis ploughing through the wet on the roadway had balloons and streamers flying from their roofs.

The car-rental garage was a couple of streets away and was open for business. It took five minutes for Gaunt to complete the necessary paper work and sign for the keys of a metallic blue Ford station wagon. Then he collected a road map, checked the directions Hans Ritter had given him, and set off.

The route was south-west. The Ford purred along, skirting the Marienplatz and giving him a glimpse of the old, Gothic town hall with its glockenspiel tower and fish fountain. From there he crossed a bridge over the slow, green, ice-flecked River Isar and started following the signs for Baumkirchen.

Hans Ritter's building yard was ten kilometres out, not far off the main road. It was easy to find, a sprawl of stacked lumber, store-sheds, and equipment surrounded by a heavy wire-mesh fence. Gaunt drove the Ford into a small car park beside an office block at one end, got out, and found the main door to the building was unlocked.

As he went in, Hans Ritter emerged from a room farther along the corridor and greeted him briskly.

"*Guten Morgen*, Jonathan, I saw you drive in." Ritter ges-tured at the silent, empty outer office area. "I'm on my own, except for Karl—and he had to go out. Only the boss is damn fool enough to work today."

"I'll weep for you later," said Gaunt dryly. "Will that do?"

Ritter beckoned him along and into a small, neat, but Spartanly furnished office dominated by a large, old-fashioned safe with a brass handle. The Bavarian, who was wearing an off-duty suede jacket with slacks and a black roll-neck sweater, cleared a chair by the simple expedient of dumping a collection of papers on the floor.

"Yours," he invited. As Gaunt took the chair, Ritter propped himself against the desk. "Any more—ah—problems since I saw you?"

"My room was bugged and I had a visit from a police inspector called Dieter Mayr," said Gaunt with an abrasive edge. "Everything's just fine."

"Mayr." Ritter rubbed his right hand, the one with the missing fingers, across his chin and pondered. "No, I don't know him. He wanted to know about what happened at the airport?"

Gaunt nodded.

"But you didn't tell him?"

"That was my big mistake." Gaunt showed his disgust. "I should have dumped the lot in his lap."

"*Danke,* Jonathan." Ritter gave a relieved grunt. "If you had, it would have been out of character. But the bugging is different." He made a clicking noise with his tongue for a moment. "There doesn't have to be any real connection. The arrival of a British official in Munich, an unknown one, might interest several people."

"Like who?" asked Gaunt rudely.

Ritter shrugged. "From here, one can drive to the East German border in time for lunch—though their food is disgusting. Or again, someone might think you were interesting in another way. I know of two foreign government trade missions in town right now. Commercial espionage—it happens, Jonathan. More than most people realise."

A brief vision of Harry Green crossed Gaunt's mind, then he dismissed it as ludicrous. Or tried to, at any rate. To cover the gap, he brought out his cigarettes. Ritter took one and, as they shared a light, the man's sweater cuff rode up a little to show he was still wearing the beaded wristband. Noticing, Ritter smiled slightly.

"Nothing more has happened to me—yet," he said reassuringly. "I'm still waiting."

"The way people like your sister are still waiting to know what's going on?" asked Gaunt grimly.

"It's bad for them, I know." Ritter let the cigarette dangle from his mouth and kept his hooded eyes focussed on a calendar on the opposite wall. "I don't like that, believe me. But I told you, it should soon be over. So—can we talk about the other matter?"

Gaunt gave up with a shrug. "If it gets it over, why not? I might as well try to collect while you're still alive."

"*Ja.*" Ritter twisted a grin, eased off the desk, and went over to the safe. A turn of the handle opened it and he brought out a folder, then returned to his desk. "Suppose we start with what you might call historical background, eh?"

"The Authorised Version?" asked Gaunt with a heavy sarcasm.

"*Natürlich.*" The tall, thin man refused to take offence. "It starts several years ago when three of us came back to Europe from Africa—we had been together on a construction project. MacIntosh felt homesick and persuaded us to come to Scotland, pool our savings, and start the Castlegate company. It grew quickly—but then, we worked hard."

That part, Gaunt accepted. The Castlegate accounts spelled out the way the operation had expanded. Only in the final stages had the first signs of a cash-flow crisis emerged and that was common to plenty of firms.

"I stayed in Scotland nearly five years," said Ritter softly. "Then I heard my mother was ill—she was living in Munich with Helga and I'd kept in touch, a reasonably dutiful son."

"That's when you came back?"

Ritter nodded. "My mother died, which left Helga alone. Helga wanted to stay in Munich and—well, the idea had its attractions for me. MacIntosh, Gorman, and I had had quarrels back in Edinburgh. Gorman was already talking of leaving. I decided I could start my own business out here and do well."

Gaunt took another draw on his cigarette, then leaned forward to stub it out on the desk ashtray. "So you borrowed the capital from Castlegate?"

"Borrowed—and sold out," corrected Ritter. He took a creased sheet of paper from the folder by his side. "Whatever the records you have may say, this is my copy of the final agreement I signed—and you'll see it supersedes any previous agreements that may exist. John MacIntosh bought my share of Castlegate for twenty-five thousand pounds, with another twenty-five thousand granted as an interest-free loan."

Taking the document, Gaunt read it carefully. Drawn up and witnessed by an Edinburgh law firm called Cockburn and MacNab, it was a mass of dry legal phraseology which came down to exactly what Ritter claimed.

"We'd have to have this authenticated," he warned, handing it back.

"The lawyers kept the original." Ritter returned the agreement form to its folder with a faint smile. "How long will it take to get this confirmation?"

"A few hours, that's all," said Gaunt flatly. "Can you pay the twenty-five thousand?"

"*Ja.* By certified cheque." Ritter nodded easily and crossed the room to put the folder back in his safe. Then he turned. "Helga asked me to give you a message. She says she has a costume for you for tonight."

"A costume?" Gaunt looked bewildered.

"You'll need it." Ritter's hooded eyes showed a glint of amusement. "We're taking you to a *Kostümfest* . . . a fancy-dress ball, Jonathan. Mainly because I'm expected to be there. Politically, it would look odd if I didn't turn up. But also—well, it's what *Fasching* time is all about."

"If you say so," said Gaunt bleakly, baffled by the man's coolness.

"As I told you, Anna and Karl are going to one of the

village celebrations—Anna's people are farmers. But you'll join Helga and me for a meal in town, then go on from there to the *Kostümfest*." Ritter's lips twisted oddly. "Each year, the carnival has a central theme, Jonathan. This year the theme is African—I find the irony almost amusing."

"I'm glad for you," said Gaunt wearily. "All right, what am I being dressed up as—a monkey?" The way he felt, that would be fairly close to type-casting.

"Helga's choice—she'll tell you," declared Ritter with a shrug. "But she's feeling pleased. I told her she could wear that witchdoctor necklace—and I only hope there's no one around who knows what that's about. Ever heard of *inCwadi* . . . the African bead language, Jonathan?"

Gaunt shook his head, not particularly caring.

"Most Europeans haven't," agreed Ritter. A note of wistful enthusiam entered his voice. "It's mainly Zulu in origin, but it spread to most tribes. The bead colours have meanings—sometimes a word, a phrase, whole messages depending how they're strung or the shape. White for love, yellow for wealth, pink for poverty—or black for darkness and separation."

"What's the message in the witchdoctor necklace?" asked Gaunt, still only mildly interested.

"Ach, some sexually rude things in anyone's language," chuckled Ritter. "But I'm not telling Helga that. For the rest —well, there's a full alphabet with regional variations. Size and shape of bead, all these things matter. The Swazis have a small pink bead that can only be worn by kings, the Venda tribe own a pale blue bead that is unique, centuries old." He sucked his lips wisely. "Your Africans didn't need to write letters. They just strung a few beads together, handed the string to a runner, and a message was on its way."

"How about your wristband?" asked Gaunt softly.

"No, only my name is on it, in bead language." Ritter shook his head firmly. "Call it a kind of identity disc."

"You said there were five made," mused Gaunt, watching him closely. "You, MacIntosh, Gorman—three. Who were the other two?"

"Comrades." Ritter stopped there with a sudden frown and seemed to be listening. Then Gaunt heard for himself—the sound of slow, dragging footsteps outside the room, coming towards them. The footsteps stopped.

"Hans—" The voice outside was little more than a weak croak.

Two long, fast strides took Ritter to the door. His eyes widened, and he dived out. Springing up, Gaunt started to follow him—and was in time to help Ritter as he returned, half-carrying the mud-covered, groaning figure of Karl Strobel.

Between them they got the small, dark man settled in a chair. He slumped back and Gaunt winced. At first glance, Karl Strobel looked as though he'd been hit by a wall. His mouth was bloody, one eye was half-swollen, drying blood mixed with mud smeared from a gash in his scalp, and his clothes were torn.

"Karl"—Ritter stooped over his cousin urgently—"*was ist los*, what happened?"

"Give him a drink first," said Gaunt sharply. "He needs it."

"Brandy." Nodding, Ritter sprang to a cupboard and filled a glass from a bottle. He brought the glass over, held it to Strobel's lips, and though some of the liquor spilled, most of it got down. The man coughed, moaned again, then looked up dully.

"*Danke*," he managed painfully. "Hans, they said I was to tell you to—to be ready tomorrow."

"Who said?" Ritter gripped him by the shoulders.

"Two men." Strobel made it a groan. "As I got back—back to the yard. They were waiting. They—I had no chance, Hans. Then they drove off, in a car."

"A black VW?" asked Gaunt, leaning closer.

Strobel nodded.

"What did they look like?" persisted Gaunt. "Did one have fair hair and a leather coat?"

"*Ja*. The other—I don't know." Strobel shook his head in a slow, bewildered style. "They—it was too quick, Herr Gaunt."

Ritter looked at Gaunt and asked quietly, "The two from the airport?"

Gaunt nodded. "And the same car. Or that's how it sounds."

"But why?" Ritter looked baffled.

"They said tomorrow." Gaunt eyed him bleakly. "They wanted to be sure you understood."

Ritter said nothing for a moment but bent over Strobel, frowning at the wounds.

"Karl, it isn't too bad," he said thankfully. "We'll get you cleaned up, then I'll drive you home—"

"Is that all you're going to do?" asked Gaunt incredulously.

"That depends on Karl," said Ritter in a tired voice.

The small man stirred. "No *Polizei*, Hans—they said that, too." Painfully, he fumbled in a jacket pocket. "They gave me this."

His hand came out holding a beaded wristband. Snatching it from him, Ritter paled.

"Same make?" asked Gaunt grimly.

Ritter nodded. "This was Bernard Gorman's," he confirmed hoarsely. Then, with an effort, he drew a deep breath. "Jonathan, please leave us. I'll take care of Karl, then I want time to think."

"You'd better do more than think," Gaunt told him curtly. "They're letting you know they play rough."

"I still need time." Ritter avoided looking at him. "But phone me—phone me here, in the afternoon."

Jonathan Gaunt drove the blue Ford away from the building yard with a tight-lipped sense of fury at the stubbornness of the man he had left. Steering along the narrow, empty road, the bright sun reflecting an eye-straining white from the snow around, he lit a cigarette one-handedly and knew his own mind was made up. Whether Ritter liked it or not, whatever the risk to the tall, thin Bavarian's political ambitions, the current madness wasn't going to go on.

The only question left was whether to give Ritter a last chance to make his own decision and wait till the afternoon. Changing gear for a corner, the main road now in sight across a stretch of waste ground, Gaunt was still pondering that one when, suddenly, he had to stamp on the brake pedal.

A large grey van lay slewed across the road just ahead, one wheel dipping into a snow-filled ditch. The driver, a man in blue overalls, looked round as the Ford halted, shrugged helplessly, and came over with his hands in his pockets. Sighing, Gaunt wound down his window.

"Need help?" he asked.

"*Ja.*" The driver, unshaven and with a grease smear on his face, ambled nearer to him.

"All right." Gaunt reached for the door handle, then froze. The driver's expression hadn't changed. But his right hand now held a Luger pistol, the round, black muzzle trained unwaveringly.

"*Schnell.*" The man jerked his head in a way that didn't need interpretation.

Slowly, the Luger following him, Gaunt got out. Another gesture signalled him towards the van, where a second figure had appeared. Grinning coldly, the fair-haired, rat-faced man in the leather coat gave a small, mock bow as he arrived.

"Someone wants to see you, Herr Gaunt," he said sardonically. "Hands against the van first—quickly. No foolishness. We don't like heroes, do we Willi?"

The muzzle of the Luger dug a hard agreement in Gaunt's back. Tossing his cigarette aside, Gaunt did as he was told and was smoothly frisked. That done, his hands were pulled behind his back and his wrists tied together. The van's rear door swung open.

"Inside," said the man called Willi.

Gaunt went to climb aboard. Then he sensed as much as heard a rustle of movement, something exploded hard against his head, and he pitched forward on the metal floor while the world heaved in a quick spin from red pain to total darkness.

He came round with a dazed awareness that something cruelly bright and uncomfortably close was glaring at him. The glare stayed while he winced and shook his head and when he tried to look away from it someone immediately forced his head round again. Gradually, muzzily, he realised he was still on the floor of the van and the glare came from a powerful hand-lantern at little more than arm's length away.

"Feeling better?" asked a cynically amused voice in English from behind the light. "I told Woyka to make it only a tap on the head, but he gets carried away. Don't you, Woyka?"

The fair-haired man stooped into the glare and grinned agreement. Then seizing Gaunt by the shoulders, Woyka dragged him upright against the side wall of the van. Slumped against it, Gaunt tried to squirm into a more comfortable position. His wrists were still tied up but his feet were free, and from the total darkness apart from the battery lamp's glare he guessed the van's windows had been blacked out.

"What do you want?" he asked wearily, his head still aching. As he spoke, he strained to see beyond that tight beam of light. All he could make out was a hunched, shapeless figure. The voice hadn't told him much about its owner except that the man wasn't old and had an accent which was hard to label yet oddly familiar. "Do you always hand out this kind of invitation?"

"Only when necessary." The man behind the light paused, then his manner hardened. "Gaunt, what's your business with Hans Ritter?"

"I thought you knew," said Gaunt mildly.

Instantly, Woyka's face loomed over him and the fair-haired man's fist slammed into his stomach, hard enough to make him gasp with pain. A sound like a sigh came from behind the light.

"Gaunt, I came a long way to find Ritter. I've spent a lot of time and money too—and no small-time British civil servant is going to be allowed to hold things up now. What's your interest?"

"Ritter owes us money, I'm collecting it," said Gaunt tiredly.

"That's what it said in your file," agreed the voice. The hand-lamp wavered for a moment, then firmed again. "You brought two wristbands for him, didn't you?"

"Yes, and now he has three." Gaunt shrugged bleakly. "Your name wouldn't happen to be Gorman, would it?"

There was a chuckle. "Bernie Gorman died in a plane crash, so let's stop wasting time. What do you know about Rionga Chiba?"

"Never heard of him," said Gaunt truthfully.

He heard a sound like a sigh. "Woyka."

Again a fist slammed into his stomach and he doubled up under the impact.

"You still say you've never heard of Rionga Chiba?" asked the man behind the light.

Unable to speak, Gaunt forced a nod. It brought a doubtful grunt, then another pause.

"You'd better mean that," said the voice at last. "Now listen to me. Ritter knows what this is about and he's staying quiet. If he shows sense, more sense than—than a late friend of his—he can stay alive to play politics or anything else he wants. You understand?"

"I'm trying," agreed Gaunt.

"Right. You'll keep your mouth shut—or be killed." The threat came in flat, matter-of-fact fashion. "Woyka and Willi would happily do that now, and you'd just vanish. It can still happen—if you make it necessary. On the other hand, don't interfere and there might even be a little present in it for you. Call it a token of gratitude. What do you say to that?"

"Good-bye, Hans Ritter," agreed Gaunt slowly. "But—can I wrap up our business with him?"

"You'll have twenty-four hours. But we'll be watching," said his inquisitor curtly. "Willi—get rid of him."

Suddenly, something coarse and thick was pulled over his

head and down to his chin. Blinded, Gaunt heard a squeak of
hinges and he was dragged along the van floor. Hands stead-
ied him as he half-fell, then he was standing on firm ground.
A knife sawed briefly at the ropes round his wrists and they
came loose.

"*Auf Wiedersehen*, Herr Gaunt," murmured Willi in his
ear, then a push sent him sprawling on cold, wet snow.

The van engine started up as he struggled to remove the
sacking hood from his head. He heard the doors bang shut
and the van begin to pull away, then the hood came free. On
his knees, he watched the grey vehicle gather speed and disappear along the road.

Slowly, Gaunt got to his feet and looked around. The road
was a narrow, tree-lined lane he'd never seen before, there
wasn't a house or a living soul in sight—and his hired Ford
was parked just a few yards away.

His head still throbbing, he got over to the car, opened the
driver's door, and flopped down behind the wheel. The ignition keys were still in the switch and he started the engine
and set the heater going. Then he sat still, letting the blast of
warm air take over for a spell.

At last, he pulled himself upright and set the car moving.
Three kilometres along, the track joined a larger road and he
took a chance on turning left. The road led to another junction, where there was a signpost for Munich.

For the first time, Gaunt glanced at his watch. Only half an
hour had passed since he'd left Hans Ritter's yard. Grimacing,
he put the Ford in gear again and in another twenty minutes
he pulled in at a meter space outside the Peulhoff Hotel.

Inside the hotel, he went straight to the bar and had two
large whiskies in quick succession. They made him feel better
and, collecting his key, he went up to his room, where he
dropped down on the bed with a sigh. After thinking for a
moment, he rolled over on the covers and reached for the
telephone. But as his hand touched it he stopped, remembering the electronic bug.

Getting up, he made a fresh inspection of the room. Then, satisfied, he sat on the bed again, lifted the receiver, dialled the hotel switchboard, and asked the operation for an international call. It took a twelve-figure group of numbers to make the S.T.D. connection from Germany to a British number but seconds later he was through to the Remembrancer's Office in Edinburgh and Henry Falconer came on the line.

"Henry, I've got problems out here," said Gaunt without preliminaries.

"That doesn't make you unique," answered Falconer with a polite indifference. The senior administrative assistant sounded as if he was having a bad day. "Is Ritter being difficult?"

"You might start it that way." Gaunt grimaced at the mouthpiece. "He also has a copy loan agreement that looks genuine and says twenty-five thousand pounds—not our fifty. The original is with a law firm, Cockburn and MacNab. Know them?"

"I've played golf with MacNab—once," said Falconer with a note of distaste. "There are pleasanter people around, and there's even a rumour he votes Liberal. But, yes, I can check it out and call you back."

"You can do more than that," said Gaunt grimly. "Henry, do the police really think John MacIntosh's death in that fire was an accident?"

"Well—ah"—there was an embarrassed pause from Falconer's end—"sometimes they do keep that kind of case open for a spell."

"You knew, didn't you?" accused Gaunt bleakly.

"They had doubts," admitted Falconer uneasily. "But—"

"But they just happened to slip your memory?" said Gaunt, torn between the prospect of heaving the senior administrative assistant off the top rampart at Edinburgh Castle or simply pushing him under a bus. Either way, he'd have claimed justifiable homicide. "I'm not expecting you to care that the same thing is starting to shape out here—and I'm getting sucked into it. But if I end up dead in a ditch don't look for anything coming your way in my will."

"You've nothing I'd particularly want," said Falconer morosely. "How bad is it so far?"

"Ritter won't say." Gaunt stopped and took time to light a cigarette. "Henry, it's some kind of public holiday out here. But you'd better lay hold of our local consul and have him primed to tell the *Polizei* that I'm on the side of authority and the big batons."

"You?" Falconer sniffed derisively, then became more serious. "All right, but be careful. Anything else?"

"Ever heard of anyone called Rionga Chiba?"

"No." Falconer sounded puzzled. "Why? Does he matter?"

"I wish I knew," confessed Gaunt. "Oh—and Henry, remember the white Rolls-Royce that splashed you and the nice man who was driving it? I'm having lunch with him."

He hung up on Falconer's splutter, grinned, then reached for the telephone directory lying on the bedside shelf. Thumbing through the pages, he found police headquarters, took another long, thoughtful draw on his cigarette, then dialled again.

"Inspector Mayr, *bitte*," he said when the headquarters operator answered.

He waited, then the operator came back on the line. Inspector Mayr was out and wouldn't be back till some time after lunch.

"No message," he told her. "I'll call back."

Gaunt hung up, not certain whether he was glad or sorry. But he was sure of one thing. Whatever the mystery man behind that light had hoped to achieve, the way he'd been knocked around inside that van had left him with a new, coldly belligerent stake of his own in what was going on.

Though that didn't mean he had any illusions. The men putting Hans Ritter through this psychological squeeze-play were as dangerous as they were thorough. It wasn't too hard to guess that Helga Ritter's turn might come to receive their attention as a final pressure to be used against her brother.

But if his guess was right, that wouldn't happen yet. In the same way, he himself was likely to be given at least a brief breathing space while these men watched for signs of his reaction to their threats.

With luck, that might be time enough to counter them. He already had an idea or two of his own shaping, and though they weren't much more than starting points it might not take much for a positive way to emerge from them.

Going over to the switch panel by the bed, he pressed the button for the room maid. She arrived a minute later, the same blond, buxom girl he'd seen earlier.

"*Fräulein*, were you on duty for this floor last night?" he asked.

"*Ja.*" She nodded cautiously. "If there is something wrong, Herr Gaunt—"

"You tell me," he invited flatly. "You made down my bed and changed the towels, right?"

She nodded again, but with a trace of alarm on her face.

"How about afterwards?" Gaunt demanded quietly. "Did you happen to leave your pass key lying around for someone to borrow?"

"*Nein.*" The girl flushed scarlet, then, as Gaunt stayed silent, watching her grimly, she moistened her lips. "Please, Herr Gaunt, if the hotel *Direktor* was to hear of this—"

"You'd be in trouble," agreed Gaunt softly. "But he won't, if I get the truth."

She clasped her hands tightly together. "I—I didn't fix your room last night. It—it was Johann. He offered to finish the rooms so I could get off early."

"Who's Johann?"

"One of our *Nachtportiers*. He—if you want to see him, he comes on duty at two this afternoon," she said eagerly.

"I'll see him," said Gaunt grimly. "But you won't talk to him first. Do you understand?"

She swallowed hard, nodded, then began to back towards the door.

"How much did he pay you?" asked Gaunt suddenly.

"Thirty marks—" the girl answered without thinking, then stopped in alarm, one hand going up to cover her mouth. She spun round and literally ran from the room.

Gaunt let her go and closed the door. It was a start.

Crossing to the dressing table, he considered himself in the mirror. Under the long, untidy, fair hair there was a definite lump where he'd been coshed, though the skin hadn't broken. His stomach still felt as if he'd been kicked by the proverbial mule, and there were mud stains here and there on his grey tweed sports suit.

Not the usual public image for the Remembrancer's Office. Grinning a little, he found a clean shirt and started to freshen up.

CHAPTER FOUR

Harry Green was always punctual. It was, as he took pains to explain, part of his image pattern. Exactly on twelve-thirty Gaunt found him parked on a bar stool in the cocktail lounge of the hotel and he seemed in good spirits.

"I had a good morning," agreed Green. "Things are going well—I know the signs."

"You mean you'll get the contract?" asked Gaunt, nursing the second drink the fat man had bought him in under five minutes.

Green winked and laid a finger against the side of his fleshy nose. "Tomorrow—or the day after, at the latest. I've booked my flight home for Wednesday afternoon." Then he gave a casual leer which was meant to be a friendly grin. "I saw you talking with an American major this morning, after you left me. Is he a friend of yours?"

"We've some mutual interests," said Gaunt carefully.

"Uh-huh." Green nodded wisely. "Supply and Administration—I know him, too." A slight frown crossed his face. "But he's not exactly the co-operative type."

"We get along," said Gaunt mildly. Then, deliberately, he added, "He said you're high in the running for the computer deal."

"Yes." Green's eyes narrowed, then he nodded, impressed. "You know what goes on, like I thought. What else did he say?"

Gaunt shook his head.

"Careful, too." Green's grin widened. Getting down from the bar stool, he slapped his stomach. "Come on, lunch."

They ate in the Peulhoff's restaurant, Green choosing the courses and wine with gourmet care. Along the way, in deceptively casual style, he pumped Gaunt steadily about his background and Gaunt obliged, pitching his manner from apparent initial reticence to a gradual opening out. It wasn't too difficult to use truth as a background for a fictional off-shoot. By the time they'd reached coffee, he had Green believing that he filled a Civil Service liaison role in vetting civilian tenders for Ministry of Defence contracts.

"Like I thought, again." Green leaned across the table, his voice confidential. "So you and me, we're on opposite sides of the fence—but that can mean friendly advice at times, eh?" He paused, then added quickly, "Just to make life easier all round—not breaking any rules but maybe just bending them a little, eh?"

"How much is it worth?" asked Gaunt softly.

Green blinked, his expression freezing for a moment. Then his mouth twisted slightly and he nodded.

"Let's say you wouldn't have to worry about your pension rights. I operate cash-and-carry style."

"Like on this Viped deal?"

Wincing, Green took a hasty glance around the other tables. "Maybe." He moistened his lips. "Look, let's leave that sort of question till you start delivering."

"Sorry." Gaunt nodded a mild apology. "I was interested. I—uh—sometimes nibble at the stock market, that's all. The right contract can do a lot of good to a share price."

"Particularly if you know early enough." Green relaxed and gave a sardonic chuckle. "Hell, you're a bigger crook than I am—and I like that. So I'll tell you this much—don't touch Viped stock, even if they get the order."

"You mean this Trellux firm is a better bet?" Gaunt frowned.

"No." Green winked heavily. "Just don't buy Viped—that's your starter, and don't turn greedy on me."

Turning, he snapped his fingers for the bill.

Gaunt was still puzzling over that one when he left Green in the hotel lobby and entered a waiting elevator. A major defence contract had to jack a company's shares up. Unless—unless what? On top of that, he remembered Green's warning about Trellux. Two firms, competing for the same contract—yet win or lose, they weren't to be touched.

Shaking his head, he pressed the button for his floor and the elevator doors began to slide shut. An instant later he had his finger at the panel again, stabbing the door-arrest button, as a voice sounded outside in the lobby. The words were German this time, badly accented—but it was the same voice he'd last heard from behind the blinding light in the van.

The elevator mechanism spluttered a protest, the doors quivered, stuck, then slid open again, and he sprang out. The hotel lobby was deserted, except for a hall porter and the desk clerk.

"*Bitte*, did you see the man who was here a moment ago?" he asked the porter, who was sorting luggage.

The man looked up, puzzled, and shook his head. The desk clerk, in turn, looked at him vaguely and said he'd been working.

Swearing under his breath, Gaunt went back to the waiting elevator and took it up to his floor. As he emerged, he saw the fair-haired room maid coming out of a laundry store. She hesitated, then came straight towards him.

"Herr Gaunt, if you want Johann, he is here now," she said nervously. "I—I have said nothing to him, I swear it."

"Where is he?" asked Gaunt bleakly.

She pointed down the corridor. "Delivering a guest's luggage. He'll be back in a moment."

"Right." Gaunt considered the laundry storeroom, which was little more than a deep cupboard, and nodded. "You better not be around. But leave that storeroom door open."

She threw him a grateful, still partly frightened look and scurried off. Staying where he was, Gaunt faced the elevators again as if waiting for one to arrive and lit a cigarette. He heard footsteps approaching, footsteps that slowed, then came on again, confidently. The man was close before he turned.

"Johann?" he asked.

"*Ja.*" The hall porter, a thin, youngish man with dark, heavily oiled hair and long sideburns, forced a grin on his sallow face, but looked uneasy.

"Here." Gaunt beckoned him closer—then grabbed him one-handed by the front of his shirt. Hauling the man along with him, he reached the laundry store, pushed him in, followed, then closed the door behind them.

"Right," he said softly. "We're going to have a talk—a quiet talk. Start shouting, and I'll beat your head in. Understand?"

Trembling, unable to speak, Johann managed to nod.

"You were in my room last night."

"*Ja,* Herr Gaunt, but—"

"You were in my room," Gaunt cut him short. "Who else was there?"

The man made a sudden dive towards the door. Gaunt caught him easily, swung him back, then threw him bodily to the back of the cupboard where he collided with a row of shelves stacked with bedding.

"Who else?" asked Gaunt again.

A quick nervous headshake came from the porter, who stayed cowering at the back of the cupboard.

"You can tell me, or the *Polizei,*" said Gaunt in a voice like crushed ice. "But you're going to tell, believe me."

"*Nein. Bitte,* Herr Gaunt—" The man spread his hands appealingly. But as his arms moved, the right hand suddenly grabbed a bottle of cleaning fluid and he came for Gaunt, swinging it like a club.

Gaunt's left hand caught the man's wrist before the blow could fall. In a smooth, unbroken rhythm his right fist slammed him just on the belt-line. Giving a whoop of pain,

Johann let the bottle fall and sank to the floor, doubling up and clutching his middle.

"Who else was there?" demanded Gaunt for the third time, flicking the bottle into a corner with his foot. He balled his fist again significantly as the sallow, fear- and pain-twisted face looked up. "Your last chance—I mean it."

"His—his name is Peter Vass." The name came like a moan, the night porter still sobbing as he clutched his middle. "He—he said he just wanted to see some papers you had, Herr Gaunt. That nothing would be taken."

Gaunt gave a short, curt nod. "How did Vass make contact with you?"

"*Ich weiss nicht* . . . I don't know," said the man desperately.

"No?" Gaunt yanked him to his feet, shoved him hard back against the wall, and held him there. "Try again."

"I—I have contacts outside," blurted the porter in haste. "He said a friend told him my name."

"And that this was your regular sideline?" Gaunt considered him with disgust. "What do you know about Vass?"

"He is a *Holländer* I think." The trembling figure seemed trapped between two fears. "A big man, Herr Gaunt. Not tall, but big, and he dresses well. He—he said he would finish me if I talked."

"Like I will if you don't," said Gaunt softly. "What else?"

"Grey hair, but cut short like an American, and he wears spectacles." Johann moistened his lips. "He—he came back this afternoon and said he wanted to know anything I could find out about you."

"How would you contact him?"

The man swallowed hard. "He said he would contact me, Herr Gaunt."

For a long, silent minute Gaunt stood tight-lipped. He had a name now, a name and the start of a picture. It was a lot better than nothing. A Dutchman named Vass . . .

"I owe you something, Johann," said Gaunt mildly.

He hit the trembling man once, hard, on the jaw. As Johann went over backwards against the linen, Gaunt turned and left.

The telephone call from Edinburgh came through at 2:30 P.M., which meant Henry Falconer had taken his usual length of lunch break. Gaunt stopped prowling his room as the telephone rang, scooped up the receiver, and grinned at the slightly surprised note in the senior administrative assistant's voice. Alexander Bell, the man who invented the telephone, might have been born in Edinburgh but Falconer still wasn't prepared to completely trust what happened when you dialled a number.

"No need to shout, Henry," he soothed as Falconer's voice bellowed another hopeful "hello" in his ear. "I can hear you. Any luck with that law firm?"

"It depends what you mean by luck," said Falconer, moderating his voice to a more reasonable level. "I've seen the original of that agreement Ritter told you about. He's right—all we can collect from him is twenty-five thousand." He brightened a little. "Still, that'll square the outstanding debts and our expenses—it's better than nothing. How soon can you collect?"

"It could take a couple of days." Briefly, Gaunt told him why and heard Falconer sigh.

"You outside people always have the easy end of it," came the complaint over the line. "If you could see what's lying on my desk—"

"Not that secretary again, Henry?" Gaunt grinned at the outraged splutter that reached him. "All right, you're overdue a nice metal in the Honours List. But what about that name I gave you—Rionga Chiba?"

"I found his obituary," said Falconer curtly.

"You mean he's dead?" Gaunt's grip on the receiver tightened.

"Exactly," countered Falconer sourly. "He was an African politician—a junior minister in the Yabanzan Government until six months ago. Then there was an army takeover and he got in the way of a hand grenade."

Gaunt swore under his breath. "How about before then?"

"Not much known. Chiba just appeared on their political scene in a previous takeover. There's one story that he'd been in jail, another that he was a guerrilla fighter who came out of the jungle—neither reliable." Falconer's disinterest was plain. "I can't see much connection, can you?"

"There might be," said Gaunt slowly. "Thanks anyway, Henry."

He said good-bye, hung up, then crossed to the window and frowned down at the traffic in the street far below. So it went back to Africa again—back to Africa, back to another dead man. And Hans Ritter had said he had believed he was the only one of the original five wristband wearers still alive.

Like a big, red beetle, a decorated fire engine was trundling through the traffic below on some *Fasching* errand. Gaunt watched it absently. The whole of Munich was building its tempo towards celebration. But in the middle of that celebration anything might happen to the small group of people around Hans Ritter.

Unless Ritter saw sense. Tight-lipped, Gaunt went back towards the telephone, but as he reached it, it began ringing. Picking it up, he answered, and was surprised to hear Helga Ritter's voice.

"Are you busy?" she asked almost apologetically. "I tried to call you before, but your phone was engaged."

"A long-distance call came in, from my department. It was good news as far as your brother is concerned," he told her. "Helga, have you heard from him since this morning?"

"No." She sounded puzzled and alarmed. "Why?" Has anything happened to him?"

"He's fine," Gaunt soothed her, cursing Ritter at the same time as he tried to keep an easy note in his voice. "Look,

Helga, I was thinking of coming out to the airport to see you —except I thought you'd be off duty by now."

"I am, officially." There was still doubt in her voice. "I stayed on to collect a package. Jonathan, are you sure he's all right?"

"Yes," Gaunt said patiently. "But will you stay there till I come out?"

"*Ja.*" A sigh came over the line. "The reason I called was I wanted to see you. Hans told me to get a costume for you for tonight—I've got it here. Though a *verdammtes* fancy-dress ball is about the last thing on my mind right now."

"I'll be out." He glanced at his watch. "Give me half an hour or so. Where will you be?"

She named a coffee bar in the main terminal building, then said good-bye and hung up. Gaunt replaced his own receiver briefly, lifted it again and dialled Hans Ritter's office number. The call was answered by Ritter almost as soon as the number began ringing.

"How's Karl now?" asked Gaunt.

"Bruised, that's all," said Ritter with a brief relief. "He's gone home." Then he went on eagerly, "They've made contact, Jonathan—a phone call, about fifteen minutes ago. I—"

"Was it a man called Vass, who wants to know about Rionga Chiba?" grated Gaunt, cutting him short.

There was a surprised grunt over the line, then silence for a moment.

"Well?" asked Gaunt grimly.

"He calls himself Vass now," said Ritter wearily. "How did you know?"

"Because I got a personal warning-off after I left you." Gaunt left it at that. "Let me guess it, Ritter. Vass and Chiba were the other two who were with you in Africa."

"Jonathan, I—" Ritter hesitated. "It doesn't concern you now, believe me. Tomorrow, when I see him—"

"You could end up dead," said Gaunt curtly. "Or suppose they go for Helga as another little lesson for you?"

"*Nein* . . . no, that won't happen," said Ritter quickly and earnestly. "Peter Vass reckons he has something to settle with me. Call it—well, another kind of debt. But I was always able to handle him, and I can again."

Gaunt sighed despairingly. "You're a damned fool, Ritter. If you're still alone in that office of yours, then you're worse than a damned fool."

"I have a gun in my pocket and the door is locked," said Ritter shortly. "Have you heard from your department yet?"

"Yes. We'll settle for twenty-five thousand pounds," said Gaunt impatiently. "Now, will you listen to me—"

"Later," said Ritter firmly. "Now stop worrying—nothing's going to happen. I'm a politician, Jonathan—I know how to gauge people."

The line clicked as he hung up. The receiver still in his hand, Gaunt swore softly under his breath at the mule-headed stubbornness of the man.

He lit a cigarette, then tried calling police headquarters again. Inspector Mayr was still out, and his office remained vague about when he'd be back.

"Tell him a Herr Gaunt called," he said wearily. "I'll try to contact him later."

Then he hung up, stubbed the newly lit cigarette in an ashtray with a bitter, crushing force, and headed out towards his car.

The road to the airport was clear of snow, freshly gritted, and comparatively quiet at that early hour of the afternoon and the Ford made good time on the journey out. Gaunt left it in a space in the main parking lot, buttoned his coat against the chill edge of wind which was bringing in a fresh area of heavy grey cloud, and hurried across to the terminal building.

A big Lufthansa jet thundered skyward as he reached the door. Overhead, he caught a glimpse of a couple of aircraft coming in to land—then he was inside, among the bright lights, the warmth, and the soft taped music. A few small groups of departing travellers were queueing at the check-in desks, a squad of porters stood gossiping under a clock, and down to the antiseptic smell of the place it might have been any airport terminal anywhere.

He found the coffee bar Helga Ritter had described, pushed in through its glass doors, and saw the dark-haired girl sitting at a table. She was in a neat blue-grey uniform with an open-necked white blouse, and Karl Strobel and his wife were with her. Anna Strobel noticed Gaunt first and nudged her husband, who turned. The man's face was bruised and puffy, his mouth was badly swollen, and he seemed anything but happy at Gaunt's arrival.

Helga's reaction was different. She watched almost angrily as Gaunt reached them and pulled up another chair.

"Karl and Anna came out to tell me the truth about this morning—and what happened to Karl," she said coldly as Gaunt sat down. "Why did you have to lie to me when I asked if anything was wrong?"

"You asked me if anything had happened to Hans," said Gaunt. "He's fine—I called him before I came out."

The girl bit her lip and glanced at her companions. "If we even knew what it was about—"

Karl Strobel scowled painfully through his bruises. "Your brother is *dumb* . . . stupid," he said thickly. "Helga, you should do like Anna says and come away with us tonight. It would be safer. I could phone Hans and—"

"No." Helga shook her head firmly. "I can't do that, Karl." She switched in a quick appeal to Gaunt. "Would you?"

"People keep telling me not to get involved," said Gaunt, and saw the sarcasm wasted. "Why not go with them? It's a good idea."

She shook her head again. Gesturing to his wife, Karl Strobel got to his feet.

"We have to go," he said awkwardly. "Helga, you understand that in Anna's state—"

"Yes." Helga gave a quick, reassuring smile to the other

girl. "Forget about it, Anna. You have a more important matter to think about." Impulsively, she got to her feet as Anna rose, came round, and kissed her lightly on the cheek. "Thanks anyway."

"We would have room for you," said Anna Strobel, making a last attempt. "You know there's room, Helga." She glanced at her husband's face. "And after what happened to Karl—"

"No," said Helga firmly, returning to her chair.

Karl Strobel took a deep breath, nodded, then the couple murmured a farewell to Gaunt and left. As the glass door swung shut behind them, Helga leaned her elbows on the table, rested her chin on her hands, and looked suddenly, desperately unhappy.

"You should have gone," said Gaunt. "They were right."

Under the uniform jacket, her shoulders twitched in a slight shrug. "Hans is my brother—and it's different for them. Anna is three months pregnant."

"Your brother says the opposition have made contact again," said Gaunt quietly. As she looked up quickly, he nodded. "Somebody who calls himself Peter Vass. Does that mean anything?"

"No." She shook her head. "What did this man Vass say?"

"That he wants to talk to Hans tomorrow." Gaunt reached across the the table and rested a hand on her arm. "Helga, think before you answer this one. Has your brother ever talked about an African named Rionga Chiba?"

"Yes," she answered without hesitation. "They were old friends, though I never saw him or met him—and he sent us the witchdoctor necklace. A puzzled frown crossed her face. "But he's dead now."

"What else do you know about him?"

"Not much," she confessed. "Hans said that Rionga Chiba was planning to come and visit us. Then something happened out there and Hans told me the man was dead, killed in some kind of accident. Hans was—well, quite upset about it. But that's all I can tell you."

"Has Hans ever talked to you about what he did out in Africa?" asked Gaunt hopefully.

"Not in any way that matters," she admitted. "He was in construction work, mostly—drifting from job to job. I was still at school then, and my mother only got the occasional letter."

Hiding his disappointment, Gaunt shrugged. "Well, Africa and this man Chiba seem to be what it's all about. I got my own style of warning-off from Vass after Karl was beaten up."

"You?" She looked at him open-mouthed. "But you're not—"

"Involved?" He grinned at the overused word. "That's what everybody keeps saying, except none really get around to believing it. Helga, the way things are shaping how would you feel if somebody quietly tipped off the local *Polizei?*"

"You?"

He shrugged. "I haven't—yet."

"And I couldn't," she said quietly. Deliberately, she looked away from him suddenly, with a forced change of mood, reached under her chair and drew out a cardboard box which she placed on the table. "That's yours."

"The costume for tonight?" Gaunt took the box, opened it, and saw neatly packed layers of khaki drill clothing. "What am I meant to be?"

"A white hunter—I had to guess your size and there wasn't much choice left," she said with a grimace. "Anyway, tonight has become a farce with what has happened—but Hans still insists we've got to go."

"So he can be seen by the right people," said Gaunt cynically, closing the box again. "Helga, your brother is a damned fool."

"I know." Helga nodded a bitter agreement, then glanced at her watch. "I'd better go now, anyway. There are things I have to do in town and—well, perhaps you could use some time to yourself." She paused significantly. "I think you're right about Hans, but I'd rather not know what you do about it."

"It could be better that way." He smiled at her as they rose from the table, and added, "I'll go with you to your car."

"Thanks." She returned the smile. "It's over in the staff parking lot—I'd better lead the way."

Taking the cardboard box with his costume, Gaunt followed the girl out of the coffee bar and across the airport concourse area. They used a side exit and emerged into a cold, grey light which seemed filled by a roar of sound that battered at their eardrums. The heavy cloud he had noticed before was now solid overhead and the roar came from a giant jet which stood warming its engines with its tail towards them just beyond the car-par area.

Helga led him through the lines of parked vehicles towards a black Mercedes-Benz, which he recognised as her brother's car.

"We swapped cars for today," she explained, having to shout against the background noise. "Mine wouldn't start this morning. The battery—" Her voice died away and she came to a sudden, frightened halt, one hand clutching his arm.

They were no longer alone. The door of a black Volkswagen had swung open and the man who came out—a big, broad-shouldered man wearing a dark, heavy coat with a fur collar—had a gun in his hand. A second figure, also armed, rose from hiding beside another car. It was Willi, the unshaven "van driver" Gaunt had encountered earlier.

"Move away from her, Gaunt," called the big man. He had grey hair cut short, a hard, deeply lined face, and wore spectacles—and his voice, with that odd, clipped accent, removed any lingering doubt. This was Peter Vass. As the airliner's engine note rose to a new crescendo, Vass had to shout even louder. "It's only the girl we want."

"Why?" Out of the corner of his eye, Gaunt saw Willi coming in close, grinning. He shifted his grip on the cardboard box, offering a quick prayer. Three more steps by the man might do it—just three. "Hell, Vass, her brother says he'll do what you tell him. What more do you want?"

"Insurance on it," yelled Vass. "She won't get hurt."

Gaunt pretended to hesitate and Willi came closer, scowling impatiently, the pistol in his hand beckoning.

"*Kommen Sie*. Move," ordered Willi belligerently.

Shrugging, Gaunt made a final pretence of starting to obey. Then, instead, he suddenly shoved Helga away from him.

"Down," he yelled, simultaneously hurling the cardboard package as hard as he could at Willi's face. As it connected, a shot snarled and something red-hot tore across his shoulder. But an instant later a desperate dive had taken him smashing into the man and they fell together, grappling and rolling on the frozen snow.

Cursing, snarling, Willi tried to use his gun again. But Gaunt grabbed his pistol-wrist and forced it away, then pistoned his knee hard up into the man's stomach. As his opponent whooped in pain Gaunt used his free hand, fingers tight together, in a wedgelike blow which chopped with all his strength at the man's neck just below the ear.

Willi sagged and fell like an emptied sack, the pistol falling from his hand, momentarily out cold. But that left Peter Vass —and as Gaunt grabbed for the gun a bullet exploded into the snow inches from his fingertips. A second shot screamed over his head and clanged against the metal of a car somewhere near.

Then he had the pistol, was rolling for cover, and at the same time sent a first, answering shot in the direction of his other opponent.

Peter Vass was backed up against the Volkswagen, the fat revolver tight in his grip as he tried for a clear shot. The man's face was contorted with anger as he triggered again and missed—then as a new return shot from Gaunt smashed the Volkswagen's side window the burly figure suddenly gave up, swung round to the car, and scrambled back aboard. The rear engine howled to life, it grated into gear, and, the open door still swinging, the little black car tore away, with gravel and snow spattering from its spinning tyres.

Getting up on his knees, Gaunt sighted his pistol for another shot, then let it fall as the Volkswagen made a skidding turn and, still gathering speed, swung behind the shelter of a line of parked vehicles and sped towards the big *Ausfahst* sign which marked the car-park exit.

"Helga—" He cursed the background thunder of the big jet, which seemed to be moving now, looked round anxiously for her, then relaxed. She was scrambling out from under the wheels of a panel truck, where she'd burrowed for safety. "You all right?"

She couldn't hear him. But her lips moved urgently, and she pointed frantically beyond him. Turning, Gaunt saw Willi was up on his feet and already heading away from them at a staggering run. Cursing, Gaunt crossed to Helga and thrust the pistol into her hands.

"Get in the car and stay there," he shouted in her ear, then spun round and started after his quarry at a run.

The man ahead glanced back, face pale with terror in the grey light, then increased his pace, squeezing through the tightly parked vehicles, slipping, almost falling in his frantic haste.

But he was going the wrong way. A high wire-mesh boundary fence appeared ahead, with the airport's perimeter runway on the other side. Willi almost crashed into the fence before he realised it was there, stopped, looked round desperately, saw Gaunt coming, then suddenly took off again, towards his left.

His goal was clear. Farther along the fence lay a dump of tools and equipment, abandoned for the *Fasching* holiday. An old tar boiler lay among them, and, hard against the fence, a small mountain of metal tar drums lay piled like a staircase up to the top of the wire.

The fleeing figure reached the spot as the noise of the jet engines in the background reached a new, screaming take-off pitch. Willi hesitated, then as Gaunt came up the man shouted a curse that was lost in the din, grabbed a shovel, and threw it viciously at his pursuer. Swinging round, he started to scramble up the ice-coated drums.

Fear took the man more than halfway up the mound of barrels before Gaunt could even start to follow. Then he made the mistake of glancing back—and at the same instant his foot slipped on the icy metal.

He went down, hands clawing, feet kicking. A drum shifted, the one above it canted and started to slide. In apparent, horrifying slow motion, the whole pile began to collapse. As Gaunt sprang clear, he heard a thin cry of despair above the roar of the jet. Willi vanished, the heavy drums bounced and collided, then suddenly they were at rest again in a new, jumbled heap, apart from a couple which had rolled completely away.

The shadow of the jet liner swept overhead as it took off. A moment later, the thunder of its engines began to recede while its shape began to shrink against the sky.

Slowly, almost reluctantly, Gaunt went forward and picked his way cautiously through the ugly jumble of dented tar drums. The man called Willi lay dead under two of them, his head smashed by one in a way that made Gaunt wince, the lower half of his body hidden under the other.

Trying to avoid looking at the horror that had been a face, Gaunt stooped over the body and checked the man's pockets. He found a spare clip of pistol ammunition in one and kept it. A cheap plastic wallet in an inside pocket held about five hundred marks in large notes along with a driving licence, which said the owner's full name had been Willi Hersch. The other pockets held only cigarettes, loose change, a lighter, and similar oddments.

Shrugging, Gaunt replaced the wallet, picked his way back through the drums, then looked around with some amazement. The car park was still as it had been before . . . no hurrying figures, no sounds of alarm being raised. Then he remembered the jet taking off and understood. A small battle could probably have been fought under cover of that decibel crescendo.

But he still didn't waste time walking back towards the black Mercedes-Benz and Helga. As he reached it, he saw something bright lying on the ground where he'd wrestled briefly with Willi Hersch. Stooping, he picked up a closed, metal-handled spring-blade knife which must have fallen from the man's pockets. He shrugged again and put the knife in his own pocket beside the clip of pistol bullets. That left the cardboard box with the carnival costume, lying burst open nearby. He collected that, saw Helga watching him white-faced from the driving seat of the car, and climbed in on the passenger side.

"Let's get to hell out of here," he said grimly, slumping down on his seat and closing the door.

She started to say something, changed her mind, simply nodded, and started the car moving. They swung out of the parking lot without incident and a minute later were cruising in the main traffic flow in towards Munich.

Knuckles tight on the steering wheel, Helga drove in tight-lipped silence. Gaunt quietly used the time to check his shoulder where the bullet had burned when Willi shot at him.

He'd been more than lucky. The metal slug had torn its way through the cloth of his overcoat and the jacket beneath, then ripped his shirt—but there was only a livid brand like a scorch mark along his skin, which wasn't even bleeding. Padding his handkerchief, he placed it against the bullet brand for comfort, then sat back again and let the last of the remaining tension drain from him.

It wasn't so easy for Helga. She drove in the same tight, mechanical fashion for about five kilometres. Then, suddenly, with a sound like a sob, she swung the car off the road and stopped it in an empty lay-by. Fumbling for the ignition, she switched off the engine, then turned towards Gaunt and buried her face against the sleeve of his coat.

"Let it go, that's right," said Gaunt softly, smoothing a hand over her hair. "But don't start crying, or you'll ruin your make-up."

He heard a noise like a sniffle after a moment, then she looked up, forcing a smile.

"I'm all right," she said shakily. "But I saw what happened back there. I saw that man—"

Gaunt nodded grimly. "What about him?"

"Shouldn't we have stayed or—or—" Her voice died away uncertainly.

"Or what?" Gaunt asked dryly. "Stay around and try to explain the whole mess from scratch with a body at our feet?" He shook his head. "When that happens, I want to pick my own way to tell it."

"But they tried to kill you," she protested angrily.

"And they tried to kidnap you. Don't forget that when you see your brother." The dead man's pistol, a nine millimetre Luger, was lying on the seat between them. Picking it up, Gaunt tucked the gun deep under the khaki clothing in the cardboard costume box. Then a new thought struck him and he grinned. "You know, I left a perfectly good hired car costing money by the minute back at the airport. That's enough to make any self-respecting Scot feel things are bad."

"I know when I felt worse," said Helga quietly. "When those drums began to fall I thought you were going to be killed too."

"It didn't happen." Gaunt saw she was still shivering and put his arm around her shoulders, bringing her closer till she was resting against his chest.

Helga gave a small sigh, then looked up at him. What was in her eyes needed no translation. Gaunt kissed her, gently at first, then as her lips responded, parting with a longing that matched his own, he forgot about everything except the raven-haired girl in his arms.

A sudden, rasping horn-blast brought them back to startled reality. They looked round in time to see a truck-driver grinning widely at them as he steered his giant eight-wheeler past the lay-by, a blue cloud of diesel exhaust smoke trailing behind his vehicle.

"He's right," said Gaunt reluctantly, gently letting her go. "Wrong time, wrong place." He thought for a moment. "I don't think Vass will try anything more for a spell. Could you get back to Hans on your own?"

She looked surprised but nodded.

"Then drop me off somewhere near my hotel," he suggested. "When you get to him, stay with him—and tell him to be careful." Then, glancing at the cardboard costume box, he asked, "What time were you planning to collect me tonight?"

"Hans said about eight." Helga bit her lip. "But now—"

"If he's still damned fool enough to go, I might as well be an equal damned fool and go with you," said Gaunt equably. "But maybe we could use some kind of a safety net."

"The police?"

"I don't know." He frowned over that one. It had its own difficulties now. Then he brightened, with another idea, and patted her knee. "We'll have a safety net—one way or another."

"But—"

Gaunt silenced her with a finger against her lips and shook his head.

"Later," he promised. "It'll keep."

CHAPTER FIVE

"Herr Gaunt." The desk clerk's voice carried across the lobby of the Peulhoff Hotel and caught Gaunt as he thumbed the elevator button to go up to his room. "*Bitte* . . . could you spare a moment?"

Folded coat slung across the shoulder of his jacket to hide the bullet-torn cloth, the cardboard box with the *Fasching* costume under his arm, Gaunt went over to the man.

"Herr Gaunt, I have a message for you." The desk clerk leaned confidingly towards him across the counter. From his breath, he'd had garlic at lunch. "Inspector Mayr was here and asked for you. He will be at the Auster Bar until four."

Gaunt glanced at the foyer clock and nodded. There was still time. "How do I get there?"

"Turn right outside the hotel and walk about a block along," advised the clerk. Then, his curiosity plain, he added quickly, "Inspector Mayr came on another matter. But he seemed anxious to see you."

"Then I'll try not to disappoint him," said Gaunt dryly. He made a show of flicking through a travel brochure lying on the reception counter, then ambled back to the elevators.

A couple of minutes later, in his own room with the door closed and locked, he tossed the box and coat on a chair, then pulled the telephone directory from its shelf and checked the entries under U. S. Army. Supply and Administration's number was among them and, picking up the receiver, he gave his name to the switchboard operator and asked to be put through to Major O'Brien.

"Changed your mind about tonight, Jonny?" greeted

O'Brien's voice cheerfully as he came on the line. "It's late on, but I know this girl and she's got a friend—"

"Don't have her thawed out on my account," said Gaunt wryly. "Bill, I need a favour done—in fact, I need a couple of favours and they're both the kind that I don't want shouted about."

"Like that?" O'Brien took the warning in his stride. "Let's have them. Now if you want me to have your pal Harry Green meet an unfortunate accident, like fall on his face—"

"Later." Gaunt chuckled at the thought. "First favour is that there's a hire-drive Ford station wagon lying out at the airport—I want it collected, and there's a good reason why I don't want to be seen out there."

"The kind of reason I don't ask about?" O'Brien grunted his understanding. "No problem. I'll be in town fairly soon and I can stop by and pick up the keys."

"Thanks. I'll be out, but I'll leave them at the hotel desk." Silently, Gaunt blessed O'Brien for the way he didn't ask questions. "If you can bring it back and park it somewhere near—"

"With no song and dance," agreed O'Brien. "All right, you said two favours. What's the other one?"

"It means asking you to scrap any plans you've got to-night," said Gaunt apologetically. "I need a big, capable guard-dog around—and things might get rough."

He heard O'Brien sigh. "Jonny, you're asking a lot. You should see the piece of woman I've got lined up and I've been working on this for weeks. But—you said rough?"

"Maybe very rough," confirmed Gaunt. "I promised somebody a safety net and it can't be the kind that wears police uniform."

"I've had a dull life lately," mused O'Brien. "All right, call it a noble sacrifice for old times sake. When and where?"

"The start point will be at a *Fasching* dance in town. I don't know where it will end," admitted Gaunt. Then he warned, "You'll be on the straight side of the deal, but if things go wrong I wouldn't expect any medals."

"More likely a court-martial?" O'Brien chuckled. "All right, I'll buy. When do I hear the rest?"

"As soon as I know myself," promised Gaunt. "Thanks."

He felt a lot happier as he hung up. Stripping off his jacket and shirt, he examined the bullet burn on his shoulder again, then gently rubbed some after-shave lotion over it, wincing at the way the spirit content stung. Putting on a fresh shirt, he considered the damaged jacket sadly for a moment and changed it as well. That left the pistol, cartridge clip, and spring-blade knife he'd acquired at the airport, and when he checked the *Fasching* costume in its box a thin smile crossed his lips.

The white hunter outfit included a leather gun-belt and button-down holster, complete with a toy plastic gun. Humming under his breath, Gaunt swapped the Luger for the toy gun, then tucked the spare clip and knife into one of the bush-shirt pockets. Then he packed the outfit away, rolled his damaged clothing into a ball round the toy gun, and looked for a hiding place for them.

There was an air vent in the bathroom. He removed its grille, stuffed the bundle inside the vent, replaced the grille, and that job was done. Lighting a cigarette, he took a last glance around the room, then left.

The Auster Bar was a couple of minutes walk away from the hotel and that was far enough in the near-freezing temperature. Going in through a small, plain-fronted door, Gaunt glanced around the dull, old-fashioned bar-room and saw Dieter Mayr beckoning from one of the few occupied tables.

"*Willkommen* . . . I thought you'd be along." The policeman's pock-marked, yellowed face stayed stoney as he pushed a chair out for Gaunt with his foot. "I heard you were looking for me."

"That's right." Gaunt sat down, conscious that the bald-headed figure opposite was eyeing him keenly. "But I didn't expect you to come galloping over like this."

Mayr shrugged. "I had another reason to be at the Peulhoff. Ah—didn't you find it cold being out without a coat?"

"The word is invigorating," corrected Gaunt easily. "I'm a Scot, Inspector—Scotland isn't exactly in the tropics." He nodded at the almost empty beer mug in front of Mayr. "Same again?"

"*Danke.*" Mayr stayed silent while Gaunt beckoned a waiter. Once two fresh beers had arrived and Gaunt had paid, he raised his mug in a mildly sardonic toast. "Your health, Herr Gaunt. Now, why did you telephone me?"

"Curiosity, mainly," lied Gaunt. He'd had a final mental battle over that one on the way from the hotel. The dead man at the airport was too major a complication to go ahead with the kind of approach he'd originally intended. "I wondered if you'd made any progress."

"In finding who tried to steal your luggage?" A cold shutter seemed to close in Mayr's eyes for a moment, then had gone. "No. Was that all?"

"I can't think of anything else," said Gaunt mildly.

"I see." Mayr laid down his beer with a sigh. "Herr Gaunt, to be frank you disappoint me. You also worry me."

Gaunt looked surprised and scratched his head. "Why?"

"If I knew that, I'd be happier." Mayr took another of his long, thin cheroots from his top pocket, struck a kitchen match with his thumbnail, and lit the cheroot carefully while he watched Gaunt over the flame. "But I'll tell you why I went to the Peulhoff Hotel. We had a report of a theft—and at the same time one of the staff, a *Nachtportier* called Johann, suddenly vanished." Drawing on the cheroot again, he let the smoke out slowly, then asked suddenly, "Do you know him?"

Gaunt nodded. "I've seen him around. If he's your thief, what did he get away with?"

"Petty stuff." Mayr grimaced his disgust. "Some trinkets and a little money from a woman guest who was fool enough to leave them lying in her room. It doesn't make much sense, Herr Gaunt. Unless"—he paused again—"unless there was another reason, eh?"

Gaunt shrugged, but with a chilly sense that the stoney-faced policeman was probing, hoping for some kind of reaction.

"That's your problem," he commented easily. "But don't worry about me—another couple of days and I'll be on my way home."

Mayr nodded. "I still would like to know more about you, Herr Gaunt," he said softly. "Call it instinct. Yet"—he gave a sound which might have been an imitation of a laugh—"in Munich we usually have an affection for the Scots and the Irish, an historical affection."

"That's unusual," said Gaunt dryly. "I can think of a few places where they'd be more likely to put up the barricades to keep us out. Particularly if there's a football match around."

"The people who founded Munich were a group of wandering Scottish and Irish monks. How or why they got here"—Mayr shrugged sardonically—"I'm a policeman, not an historian, and that was in the eighth century. But I agree, you don't come as missionaries now." Lifting his beer, he finished it in a long, gulping swallow, which left a froth rim round his lips, then pushed back his chair. "You're sure there's nothing else you want to tell me?"

"If there is, I'll be in touch," said Gaunt steadily.

"*Bitte.*" Mayr rose, wiped his lips with the back of his hand, and looked at Gaunt for a moment longer. Then, with a curt, fractional nod, he headed for the door and left the bar.

Gaunt sighed to himself. The average cop, whatever his nationality, was seldom a fool and didn't make inspector on a

long-service and good-conduct basis. He'd met cops like
Dieter Mayr before, men who had an instinctive built-in
alarm system which operated when they brushed against hidden trouble.

At least Mayr hadn't connected him with the Peulhoff's
night porter. Though why the man had disappeared and how
much truth there was in the robbery story was another matter. He chewed his lip a moment, considering that one. Johann the porter had been his one positive outside link to
Peter Vass—and Vass was ruthless enough to dispose of un-
necessary complications. . . . But it had happened and for
the moment there was nothing he could do about it.

Gaunt finished his beer and left the bar. The freezing temperature outside met him like a wall at the door, and he
turned up his jacket collar and stuck his hands deep in his
pockets as he hurried back towards the hotel, side-stepping
the cheerful, holiday-minded groups of young and old who
were wandering about. Two groups began throwing streamers
at each other, laughing and joking. One rolled-up streamer
burst on his shoulders and he flicked it away with a grin, keeping going.

Then a car horn sounded an insistent blast. He glanced in
the direction of the sound, stopped, swore softly to himself,
then hurried over to where Hans Ritter was waiting at the
wheel of his black Mercedes-Benz. Ritter leaned over, opened
the passenger door, and greeted him with a nod as he tumbled in and closed the door again.

"What the hell are you doing here—and where's Helga?"
asked Gaunt angrily. "Didn't she—"

"*Ja.* She told me." Ritter gave another tight nod, any emo-
tions held down. "Don't worry, she's safe enough. She had a
hairdresser appointment." He gave a short, harsh laugh.
"There's not a safer place in Munich, Jonathan—she's under a
dryer by now with at least a score of other women, like so
many battery hens. Anyway, I had to see you."

"That figures," said Gaunt acidly. "Well?"

"Not here, somewhere quieter." Ritter started the car. "I—I asked for you at the hotel. They said you were out. So I waited. Now"—he smiled hopefully—"maybe you can wait a few minutes?"

Gaunt nodded, his face expressionless, and Ritter set the car moving. They drove away from the city centre, the traffic around fading, Ritter making an occasional uneasy comment or pointing out some landmark, Gaunt contenting himself with a nod or a grunt in reply.

Then, at last, they reached a spot Gaunt recognised. The tall, needle-like television tower and the vast, covered Olympic stadium, which had become Munich's pride for the '72 games, lay ahead. Nearer lay another vast landmark, the quadruple, linked towers of concrete and glass that were the administrative headquarters of Munich's main industry, the Bayerische Motoren Werke car-building empire. Beside them was a giant, futuristic bowl of a building that curved outwards from ground level to a flat top. The bowl was BMW's museum, a place of pilgrimage for any car fanatic.

Ritter ignored them but still slowed the car, glancing a couple of times in his rear-view mirror. Then he steered in towards the kerb and stopped opposite a roadside stall.

"Here will do." He glanced at Gaunt, then frowned a little. "You should have a coat—"

"I did," said Gaunt wearily. "But your friend Vass and his pal messed it up."

Ritter winced at the reminder and nodded. He was wearing a sheepskin jacket but when they got out of the car he produced a quilted blue anorak from the trunk.

"Keep it," he invited as Gaunt pulled it on. "I just carry it as a spare." Then he led the way over to the stall.

They were almost at the counter before Gaunt realised it was the next best thing to a roadside bar. An old woman behind the rough wooden counter swept out a bottle at Ritter's nod and filled two small glasses. Ritter tossed some change on the counter planking, took one glass, and handed the other to Gaunt.

"Schnaps," he explained as he saw Gaunt sniff the colourless liquid. "On a cold day, it warms a man."

Gaunt sipped, felt his eyes water as the first rough mouthful seared a way down his throat, and heard Ritter chuckle.

"They make it in the mountains," said Ritter. "They—ah—don't worry too much about ageing it."

"And this must be today's batch." Gaunt nursed the schnaps glass with a new respect. "All right, you said you wanted to talk."

"*Ja.*" Ritter guided him a few steps away from the stall over to a strip of fencing which separated them from a narrow stretch of snow-covered waste-land. "Jonathan, I—first, I have to thank you." His voice thickened. "If anything had happened to Helga this afternoon—"

"That's what I hoped you'd think about," said Gaunt curtly. "And I warned you."

Ritter nodded uncomfortably and leaned his tall, thin figure wearily against the fencing.

"I'm going to stop pretending," he said simply. "Jonathan, I—*ach, ich weiss nicht* . . . I don't know how to begin this. But I want to tell you the truth now, or all that I know of it, anyway. You deserve that much."

"Maybe some other people do, too," said Gaunt, taking another sip from the glass and this time feeling the tingle seem to seep down towards his toes. "All right, call telling me a kind of beginning."

"*Danke.*" It was hard to tell whether Ritter was being sarcastic. "The start is easy enough—I told you I worked as a construction engineer in Africa. That was true, but only for a spell—I was working on a railroad project in Yabanza when war broke out next door, in one of the old Congo territories. Civil war, with good money for a skilled white who was willing to sneak his way over the border and join in."

"You mean you went mercenary," said Gaunt bluntly.

Ritter flushed, but nodded.

"And that's when you met this Dutchman who calls himself Vass?"

"His name was Gervass then," answered Ritter slowly, scuffing a shoe against the snow. "But none of us used our real names in that outfit, because it seemed safer—for instance, I called myself Hans Webber." He grimaced. "Anyway, Vass isn't a Dutchman. He told me once he was raised on a farm in Kenya."

"I wondered," said Gaunt. It sounded likely when put against the accent. "Was MacIntosh there?"

"All five of us, in a special Commando section." Ritter showed a grim amusement at Gaunt's reaction. "The years change men, but we were what you'd call a heavy team. MacIntosh ran things as section commander, then there was Vass and Gorman and myself with Rionga Chiba as the only African. Chiba had been my foreman back on the construction job."

A heavy truck and trailer outfit rumbled past on snow chains, almost drowning his last words. Gaunt stared at the thin, grey-haired man and had to fight against the crazy incongruity of it all. He was in one of Europe's most industrial and tourist-oriented cities, the landscape white all around, every exhaled breath condensing like steam in the bitter chill —but for Ritter the reality of the moment had slipped back to the heat and blood of a distant, second-rate African bush war.

"Ritter—" He waited till the man's heavy-lidded eyes met his own. "You said a special Commando section—how special?"

"We raided banks," said Ritter simply. "The rebels paid us two thousand English pounds a month, we worked behind the government lines, and they used the money we brought back to buy munitions. We lost a few men along the way but the five of us usually got through intact. Usually"—he glanced at his mutilated hand—"though this happened on one raid."

"Did you always turn in the money you got?" asked Gaunt softly.

"*Ja.*" Ritter gave a bleak smile and took a gulp from his glass. "Two Englishmen tried to get away with it once, but were caught and brought back by native guerrillas. What happened to them before they died was lesson enough for us. Until the end, at any rate."

"And then?" Gaunt sensed what had to be coming.

"The war collapsed, government troops were suddenly mopping up everywhere." Ritter gripped the glass in his hand so tightly the stem seemed in danger of snapping. "We didn't know what—we were raiding a government convoy which included a truck loaded with bar silver from mines in the interior. We got the truck, MacIntosh reckoned it was worth maybe two hundred thousand English pounds, Vass thought it was more—and the rest of us only wanted to get out *schnell* with it. Because we discovered there wasn't any war left and the Yabanzan border was the nearest safety for us."

"Well, you made it," mused Gaunt. "Otherwise, from what you've said, you'd have been left filleted over an ant-hill out there."

"*Ja,* we made it," agreed Ritter quietly. "Straight over the border into the arms of a Yabanzan army patrol, out looking for our kind of dregs. They jailed us and we stayed that way for six months—that was when Chiba made the wristbands." He pulled back his cuff to show his own and touched the beadwork thoughtfully. "Six months in a Yabanzan jail is something I don't recommend."

Gaunt frowned, a memory stirring at the back of his mind. "There was a United Nations deal for the release of mercenaries—"

"Not for us." Ritter shook his head wryly. "We were special cases—but Chiba smuggled a message out to a friend, the guards were suitably bribed, and we vanished one night. Only Vass didn't make it all the way, which was his own *verdammte* fault. Second night out, he got drunk, tried to rape a native girl, and the last we saw of him a squad of soldiers were knocking him around with rifle butts before they threw him in a truck."

"So you thought he was dead." Gaunt finished his schnaps almost automatically, his mind gripped by Ritter's story. "But what about that truck-load of silver?"

"That's exactly what Vass wants to know," said Ritter harshly. "We buried the silver as soon as we crossed the border, before we were stopped by that patrol. Then, after we escaped—after Vass was killed as we thought—we went back for it. But"—his face screwed up in a melancholy grimace—"it had gone, Jonathan. Maybe that Yabanzan patrol got it and stayed quiet. Maybe someone else—but that was that and we got out."

"Then where did the money come from to found the Castlegate firm once you got to Scotland?" asked Gaunt suspiciously.

"Our mercenary contracts stipulated our pay went straight into a Swiss bank," explained Ritter without rancour. "Some of it actually got there before things collapsed. We drew it out, we used our real names again—"

"And Rionga Chiba?" A few, new flecks of snow were in the air again. Gaunt suddenly wished they were back in the car.

"Stayed back in Africa," said Ritter almost sadly. "I never saw him again—never heard from him till he began writing a few months before he was killed. He'd traced my mother's old address through the construction company records, he joked about how he'd got places in the Yabanzan Government, and I was the one who first suggested he visit us in Munich."

"Wouldn't he have been an embarrassment over here?"

"African Government Minister Visits Up-and-coming Bavarian Politician?" Ritter grinned and shook his head. "It might even have helped, but that wasn't what I was thinking about. Chiba went mercenary with me for the money. But he didn't just get me out of jail back there. He kept me sane, nursed me along—he was the most cunning, cheerful villain I've ever met."

"Couldn't he have got the silver?" asked Gaunt softly.

"I've wondered about that myself, a few times." Ritter glanced at his watch and swore softly. "Helga—she'll be due out of that hairdresser's soon. We'd better go."

They returned the glasses to the booth, where the old woman didn't seem at all perturbed by her lack of other customers. Back in the car, Ritter started the engine, then let it idle for a moment.

"I don't know where Vass has been or how he traced any of us," he said quietly. "There wasn't time to ask. But I'll have that chance tomorrow—"

"If he gives you it." Gaunt put a cigarette between his lips and used the car's lighter. "Hans, you're still talking like a damned fool—and you're talking about a killer with some dangerous hired muscle in tow. Do you think John MacIntosh didn't try to explain things to him before he died?"

The grey-haired man at his side shrugged and stayed silent, chewing his lip.

"You can't just shut it out," persisted Gaunt with a savage emphasis. "Hell, man, suppose he tries to grab Helga again—"

"Then I'll kill him," said Ritter simply. "I managed to tell him that much." He paused and drew a deep breath. "*Warten Sie*, Jonathan . . . wait a little longer, please. You're looking at a man in a trap of his own past, when I was a young fool. Will you let me try to escape from it, my way?"

The snow flecks were thickening, beginning to build up on the windshield glass, cutting the visibility. A couple of cars went past with their headlamps on.

"What about Vass?" asked Gaunt. "Does he escape too?"

"People like Vass never escape—not for long, anyway," answered Ritter.

Then he flicked the car into gear and set it moving.

They talked about it more on the way back, but only in terms of memories. Quietly, unemotionally, Hans Ritter spoke of how it had been in that bush war of guns and knives, of terror and hatred, when death was a friend compared with the prospect of capture and what might follow.

Very gradually, Gaunt began to achieve at least a new glimmer of understanding about the man. Whatever kind of political idealism Hans Ritter now clung to as his own it was an idealism which had been burned deep into him by his own experiences—burned so deep that it had become near obsessive. With casualties in the process, side casualties in a mind more complex than most he'd come across before.

No, he told himself, Hans Ritter wasn't in any way mad. He was a man who had come to regard himself as having a mission in life—and sometimes that was worse.

Just before the car stopped outside the Peulhoff he got more details about the evening ahead, times and places. Then, with a nod and a twist of a smile, Ritter watched him get out, leaned over to lock the passenger door again, and drove on his way.

There was a cable waiting for Gaunt when he got to his room. He left it lying, checked with the switchboard that there were no telephone messages, then decided to take another of the pain-killer tablets. The low-level ache in his back was building again, though that was probably the weather as much as anything.

At last, lying back on the bed, he ripped the envelope open. One glance at the cryptic message on the cable form made him give a thin whistle of surprise. Edinburgh stockbrokers like John Milton didn't spend money on day-rate messages without good reason and Milton's cable was the next best thing to a final appeal.

YOUR SHIPPING RUBBISH STOCK BARELY AFLOAT. ADVISE URGENTLY ABANDON UNLESS YOU FEEL LIKE SWIMMING AND WHAT THE HELL DO YOU REALLY KNOW ABOUT TRELLUX ORDINARIES? THE RENT MAN COMETH.

He remembered how he'd mentioned Trellux to Milton back what now seemed long ago, though it was less than thirty-six hours, when they'd met at Edinburgh airport.

That, in turn, had been because of Henry Falconer's earlier curiosity when they'd talked about the Ritter file. A lot had happened since then.

But what was going on, what had the fat, unlovable Harry Green meant when he'd said that not only was Trellux a bad buy because Viped International would win the defence computer contract but that Viped itself was a share to avoid?

It was a puzzle which offered a welcome distraction from the rest of what was happening to him. On an impulse, he got up from the bed, straightened his tie, and went out into the corridor, leaving his room door open. Going along to Green's room, he knocked on the door. There was no answer, and he tried the handle gently.

The door was locked. Temptation removed, Gaunt turned away and saw the blond room maid was standing at another door not far away, her arms filled with clean towels, her face a study of uncertain suspicion. He grinned disarmingly at her, shrugged, and ambled back to his own room.

As he closed the door again, the telephone began ringing. When he lifted the receiver, the hotel desk clerk was on the other end of the line.

"Herr Gaunt, a Major O'Brien wishes to see you," said the man with a professionally suppressed curiosity.

"Send him up," agreed Gaunt. He put down the receiver with a feeling that the American's arrival might be fairly explosive.

When he opened the door to the ex-paratrooper's knock a couple of minutes later he wasn't disappointed. Striding in, O'Brien glared at him, marched straight over to an armchair, flopped into it, and drew a deep breath as Gaunt closed the door again and came over to join him.

"Jonny, exactly what the hell are you getting me into?" demanded O'Brien without preliminaries. "You said collect a car from the airport, right? Why didn't you mention the rest of it?"

"Like what?" asked Gaunt innocently.

"Like the place having German cops buzzing around in swarms," retorted O'Brien indignantly. "There's a story they found a dead hood under a pile of tar drums and that it looked as though someone had been fighting a small war."

Gaunt sighed. "Bill, I thought you were tired of running a desk. But if you're worried—"

"Who's worried, you close-mouthed Limey basket—"

"Scots basket," corrected Gaunt severely. "Did you get the car?"

"Yes." O'Brien tossed him the keys. "It's parked outside—I even fed the meter for you." He scowled and pointed a demanding forefinger. "Now talk. What's it all about? If I've to end a glorious army career by being posted as a Pentagon lavatory cleaner, I want to know why."

"You'll have to settle for a small part of it," Gaunt told him frankly. "That's how it has to be."

"Part is better than nothing, I suppose," said O'Brien reluctantly. "Well?"

Gaunt told him. He talked for five minutes, keeping to basic detail, leaving out most of what Ritter had told him that afternoon but keeping the rest of the story relatively intact, including what had happened at the airport. When he finished, O'Brien gave a groan and lay back for a moment with his eyes closed.

Then he looked up and demanded, "How do you reckon you stand with the local law in all this?"

"Neutral—I hope. But they might not see it that way," admitted Gaunt.

"You're the most damned belligerent neutral I've come across for a while," said O'Brien. He loosened a couple of tunic buttons and scratched his chest pensively through his shirt. "Jonny, you're almost as big a nut as this Ritter character. But—all right, I'll go along with it for tonight and tonight only."

"That's all I'm asking." Gaunt felt a wave of relief. He also felt better at having had the chance to tell someone even a little of what was happening. "I'm meeting Ritter and his sister for a meal tonight, then we're going on to a carnival dance at some place called the Deutsches Theater—"

"That one?" O'Brien's expression changed to a surprised grin. "Say no more—that's the really jumping place to be tonight, according to the boys to know. But how do I spot your people?"

"I've got a white hunter outfit—I don't know about the Ritters," admitted Gaunt. "But as long as you're at the Deutsches Theater and stay close if we move on anywhere—"

"Consider it done," agreed O'Brien expansively. He hauled himself out of the chair and onto his feet, a twinkle in his eyes. "Damned if I'm not beginning to like the idea. But if even half of what I've heard about *Fasching* night is true, then both of us better get some rest in first."

"I had that notion." Gaunt nodded.

"Right." O'Brien's mood sobered for a moment. "In between times, you can do me a favour for a change. Remember what I told you about our military computer-purchasing committee and your contact-man friend, Green?"

"He's no particular friend." Gaunt frowned.

"Keep it that way," advised O'Brien, his voice hardening. "Don't ask me how he does it, but he had two meetings with us today—and it was as if he was mind-reading all the time, getting in with an answer to almost every question the committee had on its list."

"Like there was some kind of a leak from committee level?"

O'Brien nodded reluctantly.

"He's not the kind who'll talk about it," warned Gaunt.

"Try anyway, if you get the chance." A wistful look crossed O'Brien's rugged face. "Give me even an ounce of proof, and I'll fix Green so he can whistle for that contract—or any other deal over here."

No one came near the rest of the afternoon and the telephone didn't ring again. Outside, though the early threat of a new snowfall petered out, the streets became quiet. Traffic thinned, the crowded pavements almost emptied of life, and the few people who did pass went by in a hurried, purposeful way. It was as if the entire city was saving its strength.

That suited Gaunt. He caught a couple of hours sleep—not totally undisturbed sleep, because he dreamed in a way that often happened when his subconscious knew there was trouble ahead. Some of the dream, as always, was Patty, the sound of her laugh and the switch of her blond hair. But Helga Ritter was there, too, then the cold, bespectacled menace of Peter Vass's face, mixed with dark, half-formed shapes with their own vague threat and menace.

Once, he woke sweating and with his heart pounding. He'd been back on that God-awful final parachute descent again in all its sickening, plummeting detail from twitching lines to that flapping, partially open canopy.

But at least he always wakened just before he hit the ground, and when he had wakened it was over. He dozed off again, wakened about six, freshened up a little, then went down to the Peulhoff's restaurant for some coffee. Both restaurant and lobby were virtually deserted, but on the way back up he shared the elevator with a business-suited Bavarian who had a brief case and was clutching what looked like a full set of Egyptian robes. The man gave an embarrassed nod as he got out and the doors closed.

Harry Green's room door was still locked and there was no reply when he knocked. With a silent apology to Bill O'Brien, he decided to forget Green for the time being.

Half an hour before he was due to meet Helga and her brother, Gaunt unpacked his hired carnival costume and tried it on.

Helga had gauged his size well, but the image that stared back at him from the mirror still made him grin. The designer's idea of a white hunter outfit began with flared khaki drill slacks, then a wide-lapelled bush jacket with large gilt buttons. The leather gun-belt, at least, was reality when he buckled it on and felt the weight of the Luger against his hip. But the final touch, the wide-brimmed bush hat, made him feel like something out of a fifth-rate Hollywood low-budget movie.

Gaunt gave the mirror a final grimace, decided against taking his car keys, gathered his courage, and left. Other people in a weird variety of costumes were waiting when he reached the elevators and they rode down in self-conscious silence—to step out into a sudden babble of noise and laughter when the doors opened again at the lobby.

The Peulhoff suddenly seemed jammed with people, almost all in carnival dress. He queued for a taxi with a motley group that included a Roman centurian, another man in a top-to-toe monkey suit, and a tall, magnificently bosomed Egyptian princess who was swearing to herself as she made last-minute adjustments to whatever little she was wearing under a hip-length mink jacket.

She was still swearing as his turn came and he boarded a taxi. The driver wore a sailor hat and from the way he threw the vehicle around he'd already started celebrating. But five minutes later Gaunt was at his destination, a large, candle-lit restaurant, and within a couple of minutes of entering he was being guided across the floor to Hans Ritter's table.

"Prächtig . . . you look ready to go lion hunting!" Dressed in long, dark brown Arab robes complete with headdress, Ritter rose to greet him, then turned to Helga, who sat beside him. "Couldn't you have hired a lion while you were at it?"

She smiled up at Gaunt, but there was more than banter behind her reply. "Maybe Jonathan has enough to handle as it is."

"Who needs a lion?" agreed Gaunt absently, too busy admiring the way she looked. Shining like silk in the candle-light, Helga's black hair was styled high round an elaborately carved comb of elephant ivory. She wore the witchdoctor necklace as Ritter had promised, its multi-coloured beading contrasting vividly with the soft white of her throat, then sweeping down to follow the curve of her breasts.

"What do you think of my African witch?" asked Ritter proudly.

"She makes a very special kind of witch," said Gaunt softly. Helga wore a black, figure-hugging velvet dress with a halter top and a long, deep neckline. Carnival style, it was embroidered with signs of the Zodiac. "You're carrying your own kind of magic, Helga."

Helga laughed but flushed a little as their eyes met. Then a waiter pulled out the third chair at the table and, once Gaunt was seated, they became caught up in ordering drinks and choosing from an elaborate gold-printed menu with prices that would have killed Gaunt's expense account for a week.

"To a good *Fasching* night," toasted Ritter with a surface joviality when the drinks arrived.

They clinked glasses. Then, suddenly, Ritter put down his drink, murmured an apology, and left them, crossing to another table to exchange greetings with an elderly couple who had just arrived.

"Friends?" asked Gaunt.

Helga nodded with a slight bitterness. "Political friends." Her voice lowered. "At least now I know what happened in Africa—about him being a mercenary. Hans told me when he came back from seeing you."

"Were you surprised?"

"*Ja.*" She bit her lip. "But that doesn't matter—he's still my brother."

"And Vass is a killer," said Gaunt quietly.

"Then what can we do?" she said despairingly.

"Hans knows the answer to that one himself," said Gaunt. "Give him a little more time—I think he's coming round to accepting it."

He saw the hope in her eyes and nodded encouragingly. But he was anything but sure himself and the only other way, a way already shaping in his own mind, would be messy for all concerned.

Then, as Ritter came back, a raucous, unmistakable laugh

came from the other side of the candle-lit restaurant. Surprised, Gaunt eased round.

Harry Green and a woman were alone at a table among the shadows. Both were in carnival dress, flowing white, vaguely African cotton robes. Red-haired, horse-faced, and in her forties, the woman giggled as she removed Green's hand from her thigh. Unabashed, Green leaned forward to whisper in her ear and she giggled again.

"Friends of yours?" asked Hans Ritter.

Gaunt grinned and shook his head.

"Then let's eat." Ritter gestured an invitation.

The quality of the meal matched the menu prices and Ritter was again a determinedly entertaining host—though he still bobbed up from time to time to meet or greet new arrivals. Nearly always they were the kind of people who would be useful to any politician—but at the same time there was a general warmth about the greetings which showed Ritter was well liked.

They were at the coffee stage when a photographer wandered over with a Leica and an electronic flash. Ritter blinked as the flash caught him by surprise, then insisted on another shot being taken with one of his arms round Gaunt's shoulders and the other round his sister.

The photographer moved on. Curious, Gaunt saw him reach Harry Green's table and the electronic flash blink. Green didn't like it. He half-rose out of his chair, mouthing a curse, but the woman caught his sleeve and he subsided with a scowl while the photographer made apologetic gestures and backed away.

"Maybe somebody else's wife?" chuckled Ritter, who had also noticed the incident. He beckoned a waiter and asked for the bill. "Helga, it's time we showed Jonathan what this evening is really all about."

Helga had a coat to collect on the way out, a hip-length fur jacket which she put loosely over her shoulders. Then they left, and it was her white BMW coupe which was parked outside.

Gaunt hung back a moment before he climbed aboard. A stocky, ugly-faced man in a dark raincoat had been standing in the shadows as they came out of the restaurant, then had vanished. Kriminalinspektor Dieter Mayr was working late—and Gaunt would have given a lot to know why.

"Ready?" asked Helga as the car door closed.

He nodded, the scent of her perfume tantalisingly near. Then Ritter leaned forward between them from the back seat.

"*Los* . . . let's go," he said enthusiastically. "We're supposed to be celebrating."

Gaunt had almost forgotten that.

CHAPTER SIX

Drama, opera, and ballet occupy most of the year for Munich's eighteen-hundred-seat Deutsches Theater. But come Rose Monday and it transforms into the glittering annual *Traumkulisse* Ball, an extravagant centrepiece to what *Fasching* time in Bavaria is all about.

When Jonathan Gaunt walked in with Helga and Ritter, amplified rock music from a live twenty-piece orchestra was pounding out onstage. Multi-coloured banks of stroboscopic lights blinked to the beat and the three new arrivals found themselves almost swamped in a laughing, singing, dancing tidal wave of costumed humanity.

For a moment, they seemed in danger of being swept apart. Then Ritter, grinning, threw an arm around his sister, gestured Gaunt to stay close, and started elbowing a way through.

Balloons drifted down from the roof of the vast hall, streamers and paper hats were everywhere. Slave girls and Tarzans, witches and warlocks, light-up false noses, wraparound lion skins, even a stray gorilla suit passed by in a prancing, crazy conga chain several hundred strong.

But somehow they kept together and got through to the balcony area on the far side, which had been converted into raised rows of tables. Ritter, almost vanishing for a moment under a sudden, indiscriminate snowstorm of confetti, led them over to one table that was still vacant and bore a "Reserved" sign.

"*Ich weiss* . . . I know, it looks like the world has gone

mad," he shouted above the pounding music as they flopped into chairs. "But we warned you, didn't we?"

Gaunt grinned and looked back the way they'd come, over the heads of the sweating waiters who were battling around with trays of bottles and glasses.

Back home, Calvinistic old Edinburgh had never produced anything like this. As the music paused and the dancers yelled for more he tried to calculate how many had already squeezed into the theater. But it was impossible to count, even guess at numbers in that swirling crowd. A few wore masks, and all the signs were that a considerable section of the population of Munich intended having a night to remember.

"What do you think, Jonathan?" asked Helga, her mouth crinkling with laughter at his dazed expression.

"Like Hans says, you warned me," said Gaunt dolefully, then laughed in turn. "But if it's going to be that kind of night, I'll go along with it."

Ritter had ambushed one of the waiters and had somehow managed to commandeer three bottles of beer and glasses. As Ritter completed the operation by knocking the caps off and pouring the beer, Helga produced a fist-sized, brightly en-amelled medallion and chain from her handbag, beckoned Gaunt to lean closer, and solemnly fastened it round his neck.

"What's this for?" demanded Gaunt, considering the result. "Surviving so far?"

"Something like that," she agreed. "Now you've got your *Fasching* medal, you're an official part of whatever happens."

"That's what I was afraid it meant." Gaunt sat back, looked around again, and two tables away a stockily built figure in a clown costume, complete with red nose, made a happy two-fingered gesture in his direction.

He stared at the clown, then at the lanky individual in a skeleton suit—white bones painted on black cotton—who sat beside him. The "skeleton" winked. Bill O'Brien's safety-net operation was under way, and he seemed to have brought company.

Both facts made him feel a lot better. When Hans Ritter led Helga towards the dance floor a moment later, Gaunt took out a cigarette, casually patted his pockets as if searching for a light, then got up and wandered over to O'Brien.

"*Bitte* . . . have you got a match?" he asked politely.

O'Brien grinned under the clown make-up, flicked his lighter, then, as Gaunt bent over the flame, he said softly, "This is a hell of a party, Jonny. Are we marking your phoney Arab?"

"And the girl." Gaunt managed a sideways glance and saw Helga and Ritter in a mill of dancers beside the band. "Who's your spare muscle?"

"Sergeant Harrison, Abel for short," said O'Brien. Abel Harrison gave a fractional, friendly nod but his eyes were also on the dancers. "I smuggled him with me from my old outfit. Right, we mark both."

"*Danke*," said Gaunt loudly. "Thanks for the light." He started to turn away, then stopped short. Two more newcomers had won through to a table several rows away and the combination of the man's bulk and their costumes made them unmistakable. "Bill, at your three o'clock—the oil sheik and the redhead, both masked. That's Harry Green."

"Green? Got him," murmured O'Brien, then his clown make-up screwed in a flickering frown. "Who's the woman?"

"No idea," said Gaunt softly. "*Danke*, friend," he said again in a louder voice, then wandered back to his seat.

He did nothing but watch for a couple of minutes. A plump, giggling brunette wearing a yashmak and not much else caused a moment's distraction when she tripped and landed on his lap. But she was hauled off again, still giggling, by a figure in a top hat, football jersey, and leather shorts.

The music stopped and as the floor slowly cleared an African dance troupe came on, the girls in tribal finery and the men with shields and spears. Helga and Ritter got back as drums began to beat and a new battery of spotlights shone down on the lithe, black performers.

It was a spell-binding exhibition of rhythmic, uninhibited vitality and the vast audience, many of them sitting on the floor in a tight circle round the troupe, thundered applause at the end of each item. Ritter watched it all with a thin grin on his face.

"That last one is an old fertility routine, watered down," he told Gaunt. "You should see the original—*ja*, sheer spell-binding power."

"Did you see it with Chiba?" asked Gaunt.

Ritter nodded. "At his village—and a whole lot more. Don't let anyone try to tell you black Africa doesn't have its own kind of culture."

The drums stopped at last, the display ended, and the African troupe departed to more thunderous applause. Then, as the rock music picked up and the floor crowded again, Gaunt glanced at Helga.

"My turn?" he suggested.

She smiled, nodded, and they went down to join in. Straightaway, Gaunt found it was mostly a matter of fighting for breathing space and trying to keep moving. A whirling couple collided heavily and threw him against Helga. Left clinging to her, the other couple swallowed up again in the crowd, Gaunt decided he might as well stay that way.

"This is getting dangerous," he shouted cheerfully in her ear above the pounding music. "Like an assault course gone wrong."

"*Ja*." She nodded and forced a smile. But he saw her attention was in the direction of the table where they'd left Ritter.

"Relax," Gaunt reassured her. "Hans isn't alone back there."

"What do you mean?" she asked quickly.

"A couple of friends of mine couldn't be much nearer to him if they tried." He stroked a finger over the witchdoctor necklace at her throat and grinned. "I promised he'd have a safety net, remember?"

"*Danke*, Jonathan." Suddenly, she put her arms round his neck. Neither of them were really dancing now, nobody around was in any mood to notice or care. "I'm sorry—I can't help still being frightened."

"I'm not looking for a vote of confidence either," he admitted wryly, the weight of the Luger in his white hunter holster suddenly heavy against his side. "Once I get through with this, I'll be ready for a nice, quiet nervous collapse."

They stayed close and when the music stopped they left the floor almost reluctantly, hand-in-hand. Suddenly, Gaunt felt Helga's hand tighten in alarm and at the same moment saw that Ritter had gone from their table. Glancing round, he saw O'Brien had also vanished from his table—but the skeleton-garbed Sergeant Harrison was still lounging there, and as he caught Gaunt's eye he thumbed casually over one shoulder.

Ritter was there, standing at a table several rows back and talking animatedly to the group of people around it. A few feet away, O'Brien was leaning casually against a pillar.

"There he is," he told Helga and pointed. Then, as they got to their own table, he had an idea. "I'm going to wander off myself for a moment, Helga—there's a man here I want to see. But if a friendly skeleton arrives, don't rattle his ribs. He's on our side."

He left her and eased his way through the busy tables towards Harry Green, who was sitting alone.

"Hello, Harry," he said as he arrived, grinning at the fat figure in flowing robes and small black mask. "You look like the original caliph of Bagdad. But why the mask?"

"Gaunt—" Green twisted round with a slurred surprise, his breath heavy with liquor. "You turn up every damn place, don't you? What do you want anyway?"

"I just came to say hello," soothed Gaunt, noting the empty bottles on the table. "Where's the lady gone?"

"Same place I'm goin' when she gets back," said Green, with a vague, drunken gesture. He fumbled a cigarette from an opened pack and lit it with some difficulty. "Go away, Gaunt—nothing personal, but she's someone I don't wan' you to know about."

"A contact?" queried Gaunt mildly.

"Top grade," said Green blearily. "I wan'—wanted to keep her under wraps, but the dam' woman insisted on a real night out."

"With masks." Gaunt nodded wisely. "You know your business, Harry. Except—" He stopped, shaping a doubtful look.

"Except what?" A scowl twisted across Green's flabby face and the man pulled himself more upright, knocking over a glass in the process. "Now look, if you wan' things to go right between us—"

"That's just it," said Gaunt swiftly. "Harry, you don't make sense. Remember I asked you about buying Viped shares or Trellux shares—and you said not to touch either, even though Viped are going to get this computer contract? How am I supposed to figure that one?"

"Viped?" Green's scowl subsided and gave way to self-satisfied amusement. "I know what I said an' I meant it."

"But why?" persisted Gaunt.

Green winked owlishly behind his mask and beckoned him closer. "Viped have that contract, boy. A certain lady has seen to that. But"—he hiccuped and grinned—"what they don't know on that buying commish—commission is that Viped can't handle it. Viped are going burst, *kaputt*—an' there's a bigger outfit ready to pick up the pieces. The real trick is a clause eased into the commission contract that will mean the new boys c'n up-jack the price of the deal another fifty per cent."

Gaunt whistled. "And the commission can't stop it?"

"That's what I get paid for, boy." Green seemed to have difficulty in focussing on him for a moment, then sniffed heavily. "Now go away—this is a strictly private twosome."

Gaunt left him and ambled back towards Helga. As he got

there, he saw Ritter heading for the dance floor with a vast, middle-aged blonde.

"A Very Important Wife," said Helga grimly, watching them take the floor. "He may be my brother, but I hope he breaks an ankle."

"Or maybe she could fall on him," suggested Gaunt absently, his mind still on what Green had told him.

There was a throat-clearing noise at his elbow. It was Sergeant Harrison, from O'Brien's table, and he gave Gaunt the faintest of winks.

"Mind if I ask the lady to dance, friend?" asked Harrison politely. He turned to Helga. "If you don't mind this boneyard outfit"—then, leaning closer, he added—"an' that way we can keep an eye on your brother, okay?"

As the sergeant led Helga away, Gaunt found there was still some beer in one of the bottles. He was pouring it into a glass when O'Brien slipped into the seat beside him.

"I saw you talking to Green," said O'Brien accusingly, while the music from the band surged in the background.

"Right." Gaunt grinned at him. "Bill, your nose is slipping."

O'Brien swore, adjusted the false nose, and scratched his chest through the clown costume.

"Well?" he demanded. "Who's the woman? Even with that mask she's wearing I've a feeling that she has something to do with the contract deal and that I should know her"—he paused despairingly—"except I just can't place her."

"They had their photographs taken without the masks at a restaurant in town," Gaunt told him. "And you were right about the rest, Bill. You're being conned over the contract. Tied in knots—"

In a few phrases he told O'Brien, who swore bitterly halfway through and was still swearing as he finished.

"Can you prove it?" O'Brien asked greyly.

Gaunt shrugged. "No."

"We'll work on it." O'Brien glared towards Green's table.

But Green had gone, though the redhead had returned. "Suppose I go and haul that mask off her face—"

"She'd start a riot," warned Gaunt. Then, suddenly, he forgot Green and sprang to his feet.

Face strained and white, Helga was fighting her way back across the dance floor towards them, on her own. Breaking through the last fringe of dancers, she ran up to the table, the witchdoctor necklace swinging wildly.

"Jonathan"—she gripped his arm desperately—"they've got Hans."

"How?" O'Brien looked startled. "I thought Abel Harrison—"

"Your sergeant saw it." Helga nodded frantically. "Two men separated Hans from that blond woman. Sergeant Harrison thinks one has a gun—he's gone after them."

Gaunt and O'Brien plunged back across the dance floor with her, shoving ruthlessly through the close-packed bodies. On the far side, Helga pointed to an exit door and beyond it they found themselves in a long, empty corridor. It was Gaunt who spotted a stairway leading down from it at the far end, and as they got there and started down the stone steps he took the lead, dragging the Luger from his pistol holster.

At the foot, a sign on the wall said "*Herren,*" with an arrow pointing left. Then, as they hesitated, a figure staggered out of a doorway farther along, then stopped and leaned against the wall for support.

The skeleton outfit was enough. At a run, they reached Harrison, who was pressing his head against the wall and groaning.

"What the hell happened?" demanded O'Brien.

"In there—there's another guy too." Harrison gestured feebly towards the washroom door.

Gaunt went in, the Luger at the ready in his hand. Then he stopped and swore bitterly. A window at the back of the washroom lay open. Outside, lights shone dully along a deserted alleyway.

He heard a protesting moan, swung round, and gave a sigh. It was Harry Green, who looked as if he was going to be sick and was folded as much as suspended inside the curve of a wall-mounted roller towel. The towel, in turn, appeared ready to give under his weight.

"What the hell's goin' on?" protested Green blearily. "Gaunt—I just came looking for the men's room. Look, some —some characters threw me around an' left me like this—"

Shaking his head, Gaunt tucked the Luger back in its holster. Then he took the spring-knife from his pocket, clicked the blade open, and went over.

"Hey . . ." Green's eyes widened in alarm. "What you going to do, eh?"

"Shut up," said Gaunt viciously.

One slash of the knife-blade cut the linen of the roller towel as if it had been paper. Green crashed down to the floor and stayed there, complaining feebly.

Leaving him, Gaunt went back out. Helga and O'Brien were with Sergeant Harrison, who was still nursing his head.

"They've gone," said Gaunt wearily. "Not a chance in going after them."

"Hell, Lieutenant, I'm sorry—" began Harrison, shamefaced.

"Forget the 'lieutenant' bit," Gaunt told him, folding back the spring-knife's blade. "You tried. But what happened?"

O'Brien answered for him. "He followed them down then tried to win a medal by barging in as they were shoving Ritter out a window." He glared despairingly at Harrison. "Except there was a third man he didn't know about."

"An' he hit me with what felt like half of Munich," said Harrison unhappily. "But look, they were knocking another fat guy around in there—"

"Who just happened to be passing by," said Gaunt. "Forget him." For O'Brien's benefit, he added, "Harry Green. But he doesn't know what year it is." Chewing his lip, he faced Helga, seeing the tension on her face. "It's my turn to say sorry, Helga. I don't know what we do from here."

She didn't answer. Then he realised she was staring at the knife, which he was holding loosely in his open hand.

"*Bitte*, where did you get that?" she asked in a strange voice.

"At the airport." Puzzled, he glanced at O'Brien, but the latter looked blank.

"From the man you—from the man who was killed?"

He nodded. Silently, she took the knife from him and looked at it more closely.

"This crest," she said after a moment. "Have you seen it?"

Gaunt shrugged. "I noticed it, that's all."

"A lot of tourist villages in Bavaria have crests like this," she said, trying to keep her voice steady. "It helps their souvenir trade. This one, the bull's head centred in an Alpine flower—I know it."

"You think—" began O'Brien.

Helga ignored him, swinging round towards Harrison. "Sergeant, remember when we saw them first. You said something —something about how the two men who took my brother were dressed."

He nodded slowly and winced at what that did to his head. "Black cloaks with hoods, both of them. Except—hell, it wasn't as if it was carnival dress, more like they were on their way to a local witches coven, for real."

"Hagrossan," she said quietly. "It's a village in the mountains—they have their own special *Fasching* time there, a witchdance. The knife came from there too."

"Are you sure?" asked Gaunt softly.

"*Ja*. Anna—my cousin Karl's wife comes from Hagrossan." She stopped, a new, sudden fear showing in her eyes. "But—"

"Let's think about Karl," said Gaunt grimly. All at once a whole series of small, apparently unrelated memories were fitting into place. "Karl knew the flight I was coming in on, didn't he?"

"Yes." It came like a whisper.

"Karl could have planted that straw doll Hans found," he reminded stonily. "Then—well all he got was a mild beating up. But afterwards, when he couldn't persuade you to go along with him and Anna, didn't you wonder how Vass and company knew to look for your brother's car, not your own, in that parking lot?" He saw the protest forming on her lips but shook his head. "Last thing, Helga—last for now, anyway. How did they know you and Hans would be at the Deutsches Theater tonight, or the kind of carnival dress Hans would be wearing?"

O'Brien grunted agreement. "In that Arab getup, his own grandmother might have been fooled. Jonny, you reckon—"

Gaunt nodded. "Cousin Karl has been Vass's inside man. That's how I see it."

"But why?" Helga spread her hands in a small, helpless gesture. "We get on well. Anna and I—"

"Maybe they bought him, maybe they pressured him." From his own, strictly practical viewpoint, it didn't matter much for the moment. "Suppose we gamble they've taken Hans back to Hagrossan. How long does it take to get there?"

"About an hour, the way the roads are," she said with a faint hope in her voice. "But—well, suppose we're wrong?"

"That's what I was wondering," muttered O'Brien uneasily. "Jonny, isn't this the time when you should call the cops?"

"I'd rather try Hagrossan first." Gaunt glanced at Sergeant Harrison, and met a weary grin. "Feel up to it, Sergeant?"

"I owe them something, Lieutenant," said Harrison flatly.

"Bill?" He raised an eyebrow at O'Brien.

"Hell," sighed O'Brien. "Everybody's crazy. All right, my car's outside and I've a .38 locked in the glove box as insurance. But Hagrossan's my limit, Jonny."

Gaunt nodded. He reckoned Hagrossan was everybody's limit, but it wouldn't help to say so.

"Hey," said a fuddled voice behind them. It was Harry Green, holding onto the door of the men's room and looking as though he'd fall down if he let go. "Look, someone—anyone. What—what's going on?"

"Party games, Harry," said Gaunt woodenly. "It's *Fasching* time."

He took Helga's arm and they started back towards the stair.

They drove out of the parking lot at the Deutsches Theater a couple of minutes later, Gaunt with Helga in the BMW, O'Brien and Harrison close behind in a red Corvair. Helga had asked Gaunt to drive and he used the car cautiously at first, then gradually opened it up, savouring its power and handling. He took their route directions from Helga—and listened as she answered his questions about Hagrossan.

It was a small village, tucked away in a tiny valley on the lower slopes of the Bavarian Alps. But though there were plenty of other mountain villages around, one thing set Hagrossan apart. For long centuries its isolation had remained almost complete until a motor road had been engineered through.

"That way—well, the people cling to some old customs and older beliefs." She tightened the fur jacket at her throat and Gaunt heard the rustle of the necklace beads below. "*Heidnisch* . . . pagan, some of them."

"Ghosts and goblins?" He grinned sideways at her, keeping his eyes on the road.

"*Ja.*" She nodded seriously. "They go to church. But *Fasching* for them is still witchdance time, when you have to banish witches and demons so that spring can come. They—for a few of them, it stays very real.

This time, he didn't smile. Every Scot knew the old Presbyterian-style prayer for protection against "ghoulies and ghosties and long-leggety beasties/And things that go bump in the night." . . . The Old Religion and its strange fears still had a fingertip hold in many places.

"How do they feel about visitors?" he asked.

Helga shrugged. "They make their living from tourists in the summer. But they don't see many in the winter and they prefer it that way."

"Good." If Peter Vass was there, at least that should make him easier to find. Gaunt checked the rear-view mirror and saw the Corvair's lights were a few car-lengths behind, holding a steady distance. "Helga, if we do get Hans back—well, I can't make promises about afterwards. Bill O'Brien is right. The whole thing is going to burst out in the open, one way or another."

"I know." She shivered, though the car heater was pumping warmth. "But if it isn't just Hans now—if it is Karl and Anna too—"

"Then it's a bigger mess than ever," he admitted grimly.

She didn't speak again until the next road junction came up.

The final approach to Hagrossan was along a thread of mountain road, open to traffic but with a high, gleaming wall of snow on one side and a terrifying drop into darkness on the other. The two cars crawled over it as midnight came, coasted down into the little valley on the other side, and straightaway saw their destination.

Bonfires blazed at the four corners of the village. As they drew nearer, Baunt saw black-garbed figures dancing hand-in-hand around the flames—while clusters of rockets burst overhead and fireworks exploded in the dark night around the old, wooden houses.

Nobody seemed to notice the two cars as they nosed into the centre and halted at the edge of the village square. Another bonfire burned there with a regular witches coven of villagers dancing around it, men and women alike in black cloaks and hats. Firecrackers sounded a sharp, rattling tattoo as Gaunt climbed out.

"What goes on anyway?" asked O'Brien sourly as he came over with Sergeant Harrison from the other car. Harrison was still in his skeleton suit but O'Brien had wiped away his make-up and wore a coat belted over the clown costume. "The place looks like a branch of rent-a-hell."

"They're harmless," soothed Gaunt. "Busy with it too—so let's hope they stay that way." He turned to Helga. "Is there any kind of inn or hotel?"

"*Ja.*" The bonfire flames cast a flickering red glow across her fine-boned face. "Just across the square. But would they take Hans there?"

"It's a start point." Gaunt glanced down at his khaki white hunter outfit, swore softly, then turned back to the car. There was a large wool travelling rug on the back seat and he draped it over his shoulders. In poor light, it might pass as a witchdance cloak. "Give me a couple of minutes and I'll check."

He brushed against a couple of other cloaked, hurrying figures as he made his way round the edge of the square. They hailed him, but he grunted a vague reply and kept going. The inn wasn't hard to find, with lights blazing from its windows, and when he peered in through one he saw the small barroom inside was crowded.

It wasn't the kind of scene through which even Vass would have dragged a prisoner. Shrugging, Gaunt decided that he still might as well try round the back of the building. Turning a corner at the end of a narrow alley, he stopped short, then quickly pulled back into the shadows.

A large grey van and a small black Volkswagen saloon lay parked side by side in the open courtyard. From the courtyard, a flight of stairs led directly to the upper floor of the inn.

Tight-lipped, Gaunt went over to the Volkswagen. The glass of the driver's window had been replaced by a thin sheet of plastic and he grinned a little, remembering how he'd put a bullet through the original at Munich airport.

Then he glanced around again. There was a small outside balcony running above his head, extending from the top of the wooden stairway, and a light showed in one of the windows along its length. Keeping to the shadows, Gaunt crossed to the stairway, crept up to the balcony, passed a closed door and a couple of darkened windows, then took a quick peep round the edge of the one that was lit.

He drew back again instantly, having seen all he needed. On the other side of the carelessly closed curtains Peter Vass stood by a smouldering log fire. Another man, a stranger, was lounging against a wall.

A fresh explosion of firecrackers came from outside in the square. Gaunt jerked automatically at the sound, then suddenly pressed back as far as he could into the shadow of the balcony as footsteps sounded below.

Walking into the courtyard from the direction of the alley, a black-cloaked shape passed the two vehicles and began climbing the stairs in slow, dispirited style. As he reached the top, a clink of glass came from under the cloak and Gaunt heard the man sigh. But he went on to the door, knocked twice, and while he waited produced a carrier bag filled with bottles from under the cloak.

The door opened and Gaunt shrank still farther back with his hand gripping the Luger as the rat-faced man called Woyka appeared framed in the light from inside. Woyka gave a short, coarse laugh, said something in a low voice, and the other man glanced round quickly. As he did, Gaunt saw his face in the light—and swore under his breath. It was Karl Strobel.

Then both men were inside the door and it closed with a thud.

Gaunt stayed where he was for a few seconds. He heard muffled voices and Woyka's laugh again somewhere inside. Quietly, he crept back along the balcony and down to the courtyard, then headed quickly to where he'd left Helga and the others.

The bonfire in the square was still sending out long tongues of flame and sparks as he skirted it. When he reached the cars, Helga and O'Brien came forward eagerly, Harrison content to lean against the driver's door of the Corvair and wait developments.

"Find them?" asked O'Brien bluntly.

Gaunt nodded. "All of them—except Hans Ritter." He turned to Helga and added quietly. "Cousin Karl is there."

"So you were right," she said wearily. "But Hans—"

"Has to be in there, too, somewhere," agreed Gaunt.

O'Brien grunted. "How does it look, Jonny?"

He told them, keeping the story as short as possible yet trying not to leave out any detail of what he'd seen that might help.

"Hell," said O'Brien thoughtfully as he finished. "It sounds like we'd need to start a small war to get in there."

Gaunt shook his head. "There's only one door, but I wasn't thinking of using it. All I want in the way of help is some back-up."

"And suppose it doesn't work?" demanded O'Brien with a scowl.

Helga answered that one, quietly but firmly. "Then it is a job for the police." She paused, and drew a deep breath. "Maybe we should be sensible and get them right now."

"One try first," said Gaunt softly. He smiled at her and nodded. "Just one—then I go along with you."

He felt the way she did, maybe even more so. But it would take time to convince any policeman, more time to do what he had in mind the police way—and Vass would have Hans Ritter up there as a ready-made hostage.

"All right," said O'Brien slowly, and beckoned Harrison to come over. "Spell it out, Jonny. But it better be good, for your own sake."

Five minutes later Jonathan Gaunt was back on the balcony in the little courtyard behind the inn, crouching under one of the darkened windows. The light from the other room still shone out through the curtains a few feet along and he'd already checked—Vass and the three men with him were all there, drinking round a table. Karl Strobel looked sick, and the others were not doing any talking. But for the moment all that mattered was that he knew where they were.

He glanced down towards the courtyard. O'Brien was at the foot of the stairway, flattened against the wall with the glove-box .38 from his car in one hand. Sergeant Harrison was harder to spot, almost hidden behind the Volkswagen with a small package in his grasp.

One thing still had to happen. A car purred to a halt outside, he heard the engine switch off, then the slam of a door, and knew Helga had played her part. The only way out was blocked as far as vehicles were concerned.

Now came the part that mattered. Drawing out the spring-blade knife, he flicked it open, then checked the window again. The wood was old and had shrunk a little over the years. There was just room enough to slide the sharp steel blade in through a gap in the frame towards its catch.

Metal touched metal. Slowly, carefully, Gaunt increased the pressure and felt the catch first give, then turn. He opened the window carefully, wincing as the hinges creaked, then listened again before he put the knife away and brought out the Luger.

Swinging his legs over the sill, he dropped lightly into the darkness of the room, took a step forward—and stumbled over something on the floor. Throwing out a hand blindly to stop himself falling, Gaunt hit the edge of a bed and something else that was alive and which jerked under his weight.

A woman's voice screamed in terror. An instant later the bedlight snapped on and Anna Strobel stared up at him, sheer terror on her face. The terror changed to something else as she recognised him—but by then he could hear chairs being thrown back in the next room.

"Get down," rasped Gaunt as feet pounded in the hall. He hadn't time to see if she obeyed.

The door of the room flew open, Woyka was there with a

gun in his hand—and in the brief instant while Woyka's mouth fell open in surprise Gaunt fired.

He heard a howl of pain and Woyka disappeared from view. Vass's voice snarled, the stranger Gaunt had seen with them made a momentary appearance in the doorway—and as two shots slammed into the room Gaunt fired again, this time splintering wood from the doorpost.

Anna Strobel began screaming again, crouched in an instinctive protective ball in the far corner of the bed. More shouts and curses came from along the hallway—then the sound Gaunt had been waiting for, a smash of glass followed seconds later by a flat, hiccuping explosive blast.

A man howled and dived across the doorway, heading for the way out to the balcony and the courtyard below. There were confused sounds, a cry of pain which died in mid-note, the sharp bark of a single shot from somewhere outside in the courtyard, then an odd scuffling noise followed by the slam of a door.

Suddenly, there was silence again, silence broken only by Anna Strobel's muted sobbing. Dry-lipped, Gaunt eased towards the doorway, peered out into the hall, heard a creak, swung round fast—and relaxed as Bill O'Brien stepped in grimly from the balcony door.

"There's one outside," said O'Brien shortly. "*Kaputt.* He came running out waving a gun—and, well, it was him or me. What the hell happened?"

"Strobel's wife—she's all right." Gaunt was already starting down the hall towards the other doors.

They had both done the next part scores of times before, in street-fighting exercises, sometimes for real. Take a door, one kick it open, the other stand ready to shoot.

The rooms were empty, till they came to the one where Vass and his men had sat drinking. Now the window was shattered, the table overturned, glass littered the carpet, a heavy blue smoke hung in the air, and in the middle of it all lay the sprawled figure of Karl Strobel. As Gaunt bent over him, he gave a faint moan.

"Did we do that, too?" asked O'Brien uneasily. "Abel said it would be like a home-made bomb, but—"

"No. He's been pistol-whipped." Gaunt glanced round with a grim satisfaction at the brick that lay near the window. The smouldering remains of half a dozen of the largest fire-work squibs Sergeant Harrison had been able to grab from the witchdancers in the square lay tied around it. Ignited in the courtyard, then one good, clean throw—it had played its full part in causing confusion.

O'Brien vanished for a moment, then returned, cursing softly.

"There's a back way, Jonny," he said gloomily. "God knows where it leads to—all I can see is a damned corridor, but we've lost out." Then his head snapped round and he gave a sigh, letting the pistol in his hand fall to his side. "Now here comes real trouble. Half the cops in the world—"

It hardly seemed to matter any more or be any particular surprise that Inspector Mayr was first into the room. Helga was with him, then a cluster of uniformed police with Harrison in their midst.

Hard-eyed, his ugly, yellowed face a stoney mask, Mayr looked around and said nothing for a moment. Then he turned to the uniformed men and began snarling a series of orders.

The policemen scattered. Then, and only then, did Mayr cross to Gaunt, who had risen to his feet again.

"*Guten Abend*, Herr Gaunt," he said in a voice like crushed ice. "I'll take that gun—and the one your friend no longer seems to know what to do with."

Silently, they handed the weapons over. Mayr shoved them into his coat pockets, then glared around again.

"The reason I am here, in case you wonder, is that Fräulein Ritter stopped my car as we drove into the square," he said almost savagely. "She told me just enough to make it clear we had to get here, and fast. But"—his mouth clamped shut for a moment—"it seems not fast enough. Do you know there is a dead man lying on that stairway outside, Herr Gaunt?"

Gaunt nodded. The sound of another battery of exploding fireworks came through the broken window and a rocket burst high in the sky.

For a moment, Mayr watched the rocket's downward trail, then he turned again.

"This one?" he nodded towards Karl Strobel, who was beginning to stir.

"Not us," said Gaunt wearily. "Inspector, what matters is there's a man called Vass out there somewhere. There's another character with him who probably has a bullet in his shoulder—but they're both armed and they're got Hans Ritter with them." He looked past Mayr, at Helga, and shook his head. "It didn't work, Helga. But Anna's in a room down the hall—you'd better go to her."

White-faced, Helga spun on her heel and went out.

"I've men looking for Vass, and Herr Ritter," said Mayr grimly. "But your friend here"—he nodded to Harrison—"he says he heard a car drive away from the other side of this *verdammten* rabbit warren of a building just as we arrived."

Harrison nodded a gloomy agreement.

"But if there's only the one road into his place—" began Gaunt.

"One?" Mayr raised a coldly amused eyebrow. "There was —until last year, when it was decided that the mountains above Hagrossan would make a good site for a radar defence station. They built another road. It means a long way round if you want to go to Munich, Herr Gaunt. But it leads directly onto the Stuttgart autobahn. You see my problem?"

"If you'd got here a couple of minutes earlier—" began O'Brien sadly.

"*Ja*." Mayr snarled agreement and cut him short. "Or if I had known more, instead of having to try to guess. Or even if the car I was using to follow you from the Deutsches Theater parking lot hadn't been jammed in a *Fasching* parade—'if' is a big word, a very big word tonight."

"So what happens now?" asked Gaunt quietly.

Before he answered, Mayr pulled one of his long cheroots from an inside pocket, bit off the top, and spat it expertly across the room. Then, striking a match, he spent a moment getting the cheroot burning.

"With what's going on in this village tonight I doubt if anyone knows or cares what happened here," he said at last. "That—yes, for the moment that may help us." He looked round the room again and the first trace of a faint, thawing grin showed on his face. "You've a story to tell me, Herr Gaunt. It should be an interesting one—it may even be that things would have been worse but for you." Then, suddenly, the snap was back in his voice. "But I'm going to have that story, you understand?"

"You're welcome to it," said Gaunt.

And meant it.

CHAPTER SEVEN

The dead man at the foot of the courtyard stairs had been shot cleanly through the heart. The gun he'd carried, a Walther automatic with a taped grip, still lay where it had fallen on the cobbles.

"We found nothing in his pockets that mattered," said Inspector Mayr curtly. He glanced at Gaunt and O'Brien, whom he had brought down to the courtyard with him. "Are you sure neither of you have seen him before tonight?"

They shook their heads.

"The very first time was here," confirmed Gaunt.

"*Danke.*" Mayr's rough, yellowed face twisted cynically in the faint glow that reached them from the bonfire in the square. "I know him. He's local—a thousand marks would buy him for a week. He also had a reputation when it came to using a gun." He frowned curiously at O'Brien for a moment, then shrugged. "His kind always meet someone faster or better—eventually."

Turning, he led them back up the stairway to the house.

Then the questioning began. For all of them, first together, then separately, while more police came and went and a doctor arrived to tend Karl Strobel and give Anna a sedative. There was no report of Vass's getaway car being sighted and within half an hour Gaunt knew that was how it was going to stay.

O'Brien and Harrison were first on Mayr's list and had it easiest in terms of time. Helga's session was the longest. Karl Strobel, weak but able to talk a little, was the last before

Gaunt was called through to the kitchen, which Mayr was using as an office.

His own session took half an hour, sitting across the kitchen table from Mayr with occasional interruptions from other officers. A sergeant made coffee and Mayr smoked more of his long, thin, evil-smelling cheroots while the questions kept on. Sometimes Mayr was impatient, occasionally he seemed grimly amused, every now and again he pounced on some isolated fact, then, satisfied, moved on.

But at last he slumped back in his chair, yawned, and nodded.

"*Gut.* At least I understand now, or think I do." He stubbed his current cheroot on a saucer, grinding away until the end was so much pulp. "Herr Gaunt, as a policeman I must maintain an official view of what you have been doing. But"—he rubbed a hand along his chin—"*ja,* in some ways, if I had been in your place I suppose I might have done the same."

"Let's hope your bosses feel that way," said Gaunt wryly.

Mayr shrugged and gave a sardonic grimace. "They're more likely to be interested in the general embarrassment that might accompany any other viewpoint. An American officer and sergeant, a British civil servant—*mein Gott,* we have troubles enough around Munich without looking for more."

"And Ritter?" asked Gaunt quietly.

"Hans Ritter has been respected, trusted, and liked." Mayr frowned heavily. "But now, politically—finished. Though that can wait. We have to get him back first, alive if possible."

Gaunt nodded. It was the realistic viewpoint. Peter Vass, his carefully planned operation left a shambles, had only one card remaining—the fact that he had Hans Ritter.

"Coffee." Mayr filled two mugs from the pot on the stove, shoved one across to Gaunt, and nursed the other in both hands. "I said I thought I understood now—most of it anyway. The parts that matter most come from Karl Strobel, though I can't take a full statement from him till the damned doctors give me the all-clear. He says Vass first contacted him about two weeks ago."

"That's about when Ritter's troubles began," nodded Gaunt.

"*Ja.*" Mayr took a gulp of coffee and used a hand to wipe his mouth. "Well, Vass had already done what you would call his homework after tracing Ritter here. There were no delicate preliminaries with cousin Karl. Either Strobel co-operated or his wife and unborn child would suffer—permanently." He paused and shrugged. "So Strobel claims he was forced to play along, to fix Vass and the others up here, and generally help things along."

"Including passing on the word to Vass that I was coming." Gaunt sighed and lit a cigarette. "Well, at least that explains the reception committee waiting for me at the airport."

"*Ja.*" Mayr grinned a little. "Except that Hans Ritter didn't tell cousin Karl exactly why you were coming—and that had Vass worried for a time. Afterwards, well, now you can understand why several other things happened. Even the way Strobel was beaten up, which was to remind him whose side he was on as much as anything else."

Gaunt gave a puzzled grimace. "So why did he end up slugged on the head?"

"His version?" Mayr sounded cynical. "His wife—he says Vass brought them both here to make sure they'd behave. Then, when the shooting began he could hear her screaming and decided late in the day to be some kind of hero."

"So what happens to him now?" asked Gaunt.

"Hospital, for observation—his wife can go with him. I don't think either of them are likely to run away." Mayr rose and prowled the kitchen for a moment, deep in thought, hands clasped behind his back. "Vass left here aboard a blue Opel, but will probably change that. More important, Strobel believes Vass will head back into Munich."

"That's a lot of town to hide in," mused Gaunt.

Mayr nodded. "There's a general alert out now—but with strict orders to take no action, simply report if Vass is sighted and try to keep contact." His mouth tightened grimly. "Munich is one place where the police have learned the hard way what it means when a hostage is involved, believe me."

"But suppose you've no contact report?" asked Gaunt quietly.

"Then we wait and hope for some kind of contact from them," answered Mayr bitterly. "There's no other way. Vass has Hans Ritter, and he's liable to give him a rough time—"

"Like he did MacIntosh, in Scotland," said Gaunt grimly. "MacIntosh died. Then there was Gorman—who was supposed to have died, in a plane crash but Vass had his wristband."

"I know." Mayr scowled at the interruption. "All because of this *verdammten* silver from a mercenary raid." He shook his head in a sad wonder. "Hans Ritter—I was ready to vote for him myself."

Then, leaving it at that, he beckoned Gaunt to follow him and they went through to the main room, where Helga sat with O'Brien and Harrison, a plain-clothes policeman standing stolidly in the background.

"The two *Amerikaner* can go," Mayr told his man curtly. He turned to O'Brien, his manner formal but not unfriendly. "Major, nothing must be said to anyone about what happened here. Later—well, reports have to be made. But I intend to take the view that you and your sergeant acted from the best of motives."

"What about Jonny and Helga?" asked O'Brien warily, getting to his feet.

"They'll be free to go, later," said Mayr grimly. "But stay away from them till I say otherwise."

"Then we're going," agreed O'Brien thankfully. I'll be in touch, Jonny—that's a promise."

The plain-clothes man escorted O'Brien and Harrison out. As the door closed, Mayr drew a deep breath and let it out with a sigh.

"Fräulein Ritter, I'm sorry. As far as your brother is concerned, though we're doing all we can—" He shrugged.

"You have to wait." Helga gave a small, tight nod. "*Danke* . . . I understand."

Mayr looked relieved. "If Vass contacts you in any way—and my belief is he will—then pretend to agree to anything he asks. But try to delay him if you can. We'll be there, in the background." He glanced at Gaunt. "It would be better if Fräulein Ritter wasn't left alone. I'll arrange a police-car escort back to Munich, but after that—"

Gaunt nodded.

"*Gut.*" Mayr paused, looked oddly embarrassed for a moment, then came over and laid a surprisingly gentle hand on Helga's shoulder. "Fräulein, I can promise you that our first concern will be for your brother's safety."

She looked up at him. "As long as he's still alive. That's what you really mean, isn't it?"

Mayr nodded slowly, kept his hand on her shoulder a moment longer, then turned away.

Jonathan Gaunt woke at 8 A.M. and straightaway knew something seemed wrong. Then, after a moment or two, he realised it was the silence all round. Puzzled, yawning, he threw back the blanket he'd wrapped around him, hauled himself out of the chair in which he'd spent the night, padded over to the hotel room window, and looked out.

Then he grinned wryly. The centre of Munich seemed deserted. There was no traffic, the shops were still closed, the bright morning sunlight shone down on a street empty of life of any kind. The city was recovering gently from a long, hard night.

A low, stirring noise came from the bed and he turned, the grin softening as he considered the small, curled-up figure still lying there. Helga's long, dark hair contrasted silkily against the white of the pillow, one arm was outstretched protectively, and as he watched she stirred again in her sleep.

He found his cigarettes and lit one.

When they'd left Hagrossan the witchdance bonfires had died down to mere mounds of red, glowing ash in the night. Mayr's promised police car tailing them, they'd driven back towards Munich but Helga had instinctively rejected the idea of spending what was left of the night at home, with those other, empty rooms to mock her.

Instead, they'd made a brief stop to let her collect a change of clothing, then driven on. It was now after 3 A.M. but Munich was still celebrating. The police car left them at the Peulhoff Hotel, where no one seemed to know or care who was coming and going, and he'd taken Helga up to his room.

By then she'd begun to show the full strain of what she'd been through. Almost out on her feet, she'd lain down on the bed while Gaunt made a vain try to raise room service. When he'd given up and laid down the phone again, she'd gone to sleep.

He chuckled to himself at the memory. Whatever his own feelings, she'd hardly stirred as he'd make her more comfortable. Sleepy lips had managed to brush his own as he'd finished, then there had been only her soft, gentle breathing and the blanket waiting on the chair where he'd tried to keep some kind of vigil.

Things happened that way. He stubbed the cigarette, felt the overnight stubble on his chin, and went into the bathroom. Ten minutes later, showered, shaved, and dressed in ordinary clothes again, he felt fresh and back to normal.

"*Guten Morgen,*" said a quiet voice from the bed as he came back out.

"Hello." He grinned at her. She was sitting up, eyeing him solemnly, knees drawn up to her chin under the quilt. "I was going to leave you till I got some breakfast sent up."

"Last night—" began Helga.

"You went out like a light, that's all," Gaunt told her.

"That's not what I meant." She frowned at him, almost annoyed. "I—Jonathan, whatever happens, I owe you a lot."

"Tell that to Inspector Mayr," he suggested dryly. "He seems to have other ideas."

She shook her head, beckoned him nearer, then put her arms round his neck and kissed him gently. Then, letting him go again, she gave a small sigh.

"Has there—"

"No." He could only shrug. "Nothing from anyone, Helga. It could take time."

She said nothing, accepting his answer. After a minute or two she got up, took the overnight bag she'd brought with her, and went into the bathroom. As he heard the shower start to run, Gaunt tried room service on the telephone. This time a tired voice finally answered with a faint note of amazement that anyone else should be awake. Gaunt ordered breakfast, hung up, then lit another cigarette and went to the window again.

Out there, under one of those snow-covered roofs that sheltered about a million people, Peter Vass had Ritter. Comrades once, now captor and captive—and Vass also had Woyka with him.

A picture of the fair-haired thug's thin, rat-like face crossed Gaunt's mind and his lips tightened. Woyka was vicious, probably almost as dangerous and ruthless as Vass. But for the moment there was no way anyone could help Hans Ritter —the Bavarian was absolutely on his own.

Which in itself wasn't a pleasant thought.

Breakfast for two arrived on a trolley a few minutes later, the waiter's eyes roving curiously around the room as he positioned the trolley near the window. Helga emerged from the bathroom as he was leaving and the man eyed her with an impassive appreciation, then, as he closed the door, gave Gaunt the merest suspicion of a wink.

It hadn't been earned. But Helga's tiredness no longer showed. Hair brushed and combed, fresh lipstick in place, she was in the white sweater, corduroy trousers, and deerskin boots outfit she'd been wearing when Gaunt had first met her. That might have been a deliberate choice, but for the moment her main interest seemed to be on the breakfast trolley.

They ate quietly, almost avoiding talking, and were just finishing when the telephone suddenly rang. Helga jerked at the sound and glanced at Gaunt, who shrugged and went over quickly to lift the receiver.

"Gaunt?" The flat, nasally accented voice in his ear didn't need any introduction. "Vass—is the girl with you?"

"Yes." He saw Helga on her feet but held up a hand, warning her to stay quiet as she came over. "She's here. What do you want?"

"Something she has," Vass answered unemotionally. "You can tell her that either I get it or she won't see her brother alive again."

Gaunt chewed his lip. "Can you prove he is still alive, Vass?"

"I say he's alive and that'll have to do you for now," said Vass impatiently. "Now listen, because I'm only saying this once. Has she got the witchdoctor necklace Chiba sent Ritter —the one she was wearing last night?"

"Wait." Gaunt put his free hand over the mouthpiece and turned to Helga. "He wants the head necklace."

"The necklace?" She looked bewildered. "What did he say about Hans?"

"He says he's all right," answered Gaunt, looking past her and around the room. "The necklace, Helga—where is it?"

She hurried over to the side of the bed, stooped, and rose again with the heavy beads rippling in her hand.

"Right." Gaunt took his hand from the mouthpiece. "Yes, we've got it."

"Good." A new, coldly menacing note entered the voice on the line. "Now, if there are any police around tell them to stay clear—absolutely clear. Do you still have that Ford station wagon you hired?"

"Yes." Gaunt waited.

"Then in exactly three minutes you'll leave the hotel together," instructed Vass. "You'll take the station wagon—not the Ritter girl's car—and you'll drive out along Brienner Strasse. There's a monument in the middle of a junction on the way, and a phone booth on the pavement farther along. Get there, get into the booth, and wait. Understand?"

"Brienner Strasse, past the monument," agreed Gaunt. "But we're not handing anything over until you prove Ritter is still alive and tell us what kind of deal you're offering."

"The deal is he stays alive," snapped Vass. "But you'll see him all right—at the same time as I get that necklace. Three minutes, Gaunt, then be on your way."

The line went dead. Swearing softly, Gaunt hung up and faced Helga again.

"I heard," she said quietly. "Enough, anyway. But—" Still bewildered, she stared at the necklace in her hands. "Why this?"

Shaking his head, Gaunt took it from her and ran the strung, patterned beads through his fingers. Wood and cheap glass and vegetable seeds—it looked exactly what it had to be, a piece of hand-made African folkcraft.

He sighed, only one idea left. "Your brother told me there was a bead language. Suppose there's some kind of message in the patterns—a message he never realised was there."

"*Ich weiss nicht* . . . I don't know." Helga frowned over it with him. "Hans said there was a message, that there always is. But he said it was—"

"High-grade pornographic." Gaunt nodded. "That's what he told me. Do we give it to Vass?"

"If Hans is there." She bit her lip, then crossed the room to pick up her jacket.

Gaunt shoved the necklace into his pocket and winced as the telephone pealed again. For a moment he was tempted to ignore it but he couldn't, and he scooped up the receiver.

"*Guten Morgen*," said Inspector Dieter Mayr at the other end of the line. "Herr Gaunt, just to let you know we have a tap on your phone. I heard Vass's call."

"Then you'd hear what he said about police interference," said Gaunt grimly. "So what do we do?"

"Go along with him," said Mayr, unperturbed. "That's what you propose to do, isn't it?"

"Yes." He saw Helga at his side again, straining to hear, and took the receiver a little back from his ear to make it easier. "But what about your people?"

"We'll be around," promised Mayr. "But don't expect to see us—and tell Fräulein Ritter she has my word we won't interfere unless it is safe."

"How safe?" demanded Gaunt.

"I'll judge that when the time comes—if it comes." There was a pause and a grunt over the line. "By my watch, you have exactly a minute left of Vass's timing. Do one thing for me, Herr Gaunt. When you meet him, keep him talking—whatever happens, keep him talking. Good luck and *auf Wiedersehen*."

"Thanks," said Gaunt sardonically and put down the receiver. Then he saw the look of worry on Helga's face and grimaced reassuringly. "He's no fool. I reckon you can trust him."

He could have added that there wasn't much option. But it would hardly have helped.

Having been lying out overnight in that freezing temperature, the Ford needed full choke and some starter winding before the engine fired. But after that it warmed quickly as they cruised along one deserted street after another. The only vehicle they passed was a delivery truck, and the white-coated driver had the look of a man who needed all the support he could get from the steering wheel.

Brienner Strasse came up, then the monument Vass had

mentioned—a tall obelisk that was a war memorial from Napoleonic times in the centre of a square. Skirting the square, Gaunt slowed as he saw the phone booth ahead. Then, pulling in, he got out.

The booth was empty when he reached it. A minute passed, the telephone jangled to life, and when he lifted it he heard Vass chuckle over the line.

"That's stage one, Gaunt," said Vass's flat, nasal voice. "Now we're going to do the same routine again—go to Theresienstrasse and you'll find another phone booth near the taxi rank and from there it's for real. Understand?"

"Theresienstrasse," repeated Gaunt woodenly. "And damn your routine. It's old enough to have a beard."

Vass gave a noise like a dehydrated laugh and the line went dead. Putting down the receiver, Gaunt went back to the car and got in.

"He's playing with us," he told Helga. "Playing careful at the same time. It's Theresienstrasse next."

He started the Ford and they drove off again, Helga guiding him through the streets. Pedestrians were beginning to make an appearance here and there and a few other vehicles were driving around. If nothing else, the city was beginning to yawn.

The phone booth at the Theresienstrasse taxi rank was being used by a woman as they pulled up. But she left after a moment, and Gaunt was there and waiting when the instrument began ringing. This time, when he picked up the receiver, he heard a harsher note in Vass's voice.

"Remember yesterday, when you were with Ritter near the Olympic Stadium?" Vass didn't wait for an answer. "We were watching you then, like we're watching you now. No drinks this time, Gaunt—get there, park at the BMW Museum building. Then go in—and bring the girl with you."

"Why?" demanded Gaunt suspiciously.

"Because she wants proof her damned brother is still alive, doesn't she?" snapped Vass impatiently. "Now listen—once inside, take the escalator to the top floor. But don't try to dream up any clever notions on the way. They won't work."

He rang off.

When Gaunt left the booth, he took a slow, deliberate look around. Maybe Vass did have someone watching them, maybe it was all an elaborate charade designed to impress and frighten. But any watcher hadn't showed, and the promised police back-up was equally invisible. For all practical purposes, he and Helga were very much alone.

Going back to the car, he told Helga their new instructions. Somehow, she managed to produce a wry smile though her hands tightened nervously.

"At least it will be warm in there," she said resignedly. "You should have thanked him for that much." Then she paused hopefully. "You're sure he said Hans would be there?"

"He hinted it," qualified Gaunt.

Turning the starter key, he set the Ford going again on their last lap.

A fresh hint of snow was back in the air by the time they drew into the museum parking lot. A handful of other cars lay around, cold, anonymous shapes under the grey, heavy sky. The light wind had an icy edge to it as they left the Ford, hurrying across towards the great bowl of a building, and Gaunt was glad when they got inside.

A smartly dressed, middle-aged woman attendant sat at the entrance desk, a paper cup of coffee beside her, and smiled a greeting at Helga as they went on, passing a glass display counter filled with souvenirs and postcards.

Then Gaunt stopped short, even the strikingly advanced architecture of the outer shell of the building having left him unprepared for what he saw.

Five distinctive levels in height, the museum had been built by men who seemed determined to create something close to a temple of worship to the automobile. From ground level, the stainless-steel treads of the escalator Vass had described led in one rippling, moving line to the very top platform.

Then, from there all the way down again, a broad, wide ramp carpeted in a continuous blue clung to the circular inner wall of the bowl in a series of display units and platforms. Bright colours, concealed lighting, and polished metalwork blended in a way which added to the almost religious atmosphere . . . a religion based on the glinting, beautifully prepared exhibits that were spaced at carefully regulated intervals along the curving ramp and its occasional platforms.

Even where he was, with most of the vehicles half-hidden, Gaunt found himself identifying treasures which would have reduced any private collector to despairing envy. To his right was a coffee and cream 315 Cabriolet model from the mid-thirties and one of the slim, two-seat sports roadsters which had been BMW's pride when World War II broke out. Farther up, he caught a glimpse of a 1970s style Formula Two machine and an example of the cheeky little Dixi roadster with which the Bayerische Motoren Werke had launched into car production in the 1920s after a history devoted to motorcycles and aero engines.

But that wasn't why they'd come.

"Ready?" he asked quietly.

Helga nodded, and they stepped onto the gently purring escalator.

As they rose with it, more exhibits slid past on either side. Tourers, limousines, the famed 1939 Rennsport created for the Mille Miglia, then jet engines and a strange, stubby, half-car half-aircraft shape which had once held the world motorcycle speed record.

All without a single visiting admirer in sight. Gaunt glanced at the girl by his side and said nothing but knew that Peter Vass had chosen well, chosen beautifully in terms of time and place.

They reached the top of the escalator and stepped off. Above their heads, a slide projector ticked and clicked as it threw a constantly changing mural of pictures on a series of wall screens. Down at the bottom of the escalator, the same middle-aged woman was still sipping peacefully at her coffee.

"Over here, Gaunt," said a quiet voice from their left.

Peter Vass stood about a dozen steps away, where he'd emerged from behind a dark blue sports coupe. Eyes glinting behind his spectacle lenses, he beckoned with a forefinger. But his other hand stayed deep in the pocket of the dark winter coat he wore with a fur hat and a grey business suit.

Gaunt felt Helga's hand grip his arm. They went over slowly and Vass gestured them to stop when they were about two paces away.

"Near enough," he said curtly, his hard, lined face empty of emotion. "You brought the witchdoctor necklace?"

"*Ja,* we did," answered Helga steadily, her head coming up determinedly. "But I have to see Hans first."

Vass nodded. "I'm holding a gun and it's aimed at Gaunt's stomach. So stay quiet—but look down to your right."

They did, and Helga drew a quick breath of relief. Two figures were standing at the rail of the level immediately below their own, beside a cluster of cars from the 1930s. The nearest was Hans Ritter, wearing a heavy sweater and blue slacks. Face pale and exhausted, he stared almost unbelievingly across the gap towards Helga. Then, as if a spark of hope had been lit, he lifted a hand to wave.

But Woyka was beside him. The rat-like face scowled a warning and Woyka, in a leather jacket buttoned to the throat, nudged him hard. Ritter's gesture died almost before it had begun.

"Satisfied?" asked Peter Vass. Then he ignored Helga for a moment. "Gaunt, I'd be very careful with Woyka. He took a bullet in his arm from you last night. Only a flesh wound, but it hurt—and he won't forget that."

"Should I say sorry to him?" asked Gaunt sardonically.

Vass gave a semblance of a grin, then let it fade. "I'll spell the rest out for you both. I want the necklace, then Woyka and I leave here with Ritter." He glanced shrewdly at Helga. "We'll turn your brother loose later—when we're sure we've got what we want and that we're clear of any *Polizei*-style interference."

She moistened her lips. "That's not good enough. I—"

"You want your brother alive," snapped Vass.

"Exactly," mused Gaunt. "But can she trust you? There was a night porter at the Peulhoff who vanished when he stopped being useful—what happened to him?"

Vass shrugged. "He'll be fished out of the River Isar sooner or later, but we killed him because he'd become dangerous. Ritter—if I get what I want, Ritter lives." He drew a deep breath, then pointed a finger at Helga in sudden anger. "At that, your damned precious brother is getting a better deal than he handed out to me in Africa."

"The way Ritter tells it, he thought you were dead," said Gaunt quietly. "They all did."

"How hard did they try to make sure?" asked Vass viciously. "They abandoned me—left me to rot in a stinking Yabanzan jail. Five years of it, Gaunt—five years living like an animal and staying alive on food worse than pig swill." His eyes blinked in fury behind the spectacles. "What were they doing those five years? Living well—not giving a damn."

Gaunt looked across the museum's width, down towards the tired, beaten figure of Hans Ritter, the sheer venom behind Vass's words giving little cause to sustain much hope for Ritter's eventual safety, whatever might be promised.

"You said five years. What happened at the end of it?" he said quickly.

"I killed a guard and got away from a work party." Vass twisted a cynical grin. "Then I worked my way down to South Africa, and got myself organised. That took time, too, but when you've got my kind of reason, time doesn't matter— you just add it to the bill. Gorman came first and easiest—"

"Gorman?" Helga stared at him. "But Hans thought—he was supposed to have been killed in an air crash!"

"In a light plane that disappeared in the bush," agreed Vass contemptuously, and shrugged a little under his heavy coat. "The only mistake I made there was he died too soon, before he could talk. But I got the first of those wristbands from him—"

He stopped short, tensing. Down on the ground floor, a man in overalls had entered the museum area. He carried a bucket and a toolbox, dumped both on the floor beside the entrance desk, and began gossiping with the woman attendant. Relaxing a little, Vass gave a hand-signal across to Woyka, waited till the fair-haired man had pushed Hans Ritter farther back towards the shelter of the exhibits behind them, then faced Gaunt again with a new impatience.

"All right, let's get it done. I get the necklace, you get Ritter in one piece as soon as I stop needing him."

"Feeling nervous about it?" asked Gaunt mildly. As he spoke, he was thinking desperately. Down below, the maintenance man still had his back to them as he finished his conversation. But the man was a minor factor—and even if by a miracle he could take Vass where they were, that still left Woyka holding Ritter, holding him tantalisingly near and yet in practical terms hopelessly far away. "What's so special about the necklace anyway?"

"It was made by Rionga Chiba," said Vass harshly and gave a wolfish grin at Helga. "I got that out of your precious brother—though he was too big a fool to understand what that meant."

"You think Chiba got that load of silver from the convoy raid?" asked Gaunt, frowning.

"I know it—now," snarled Vass.

The maintenance man had left the desk and, ignoring the escalator, was beginning to walk up the winding display ramp. He passed a couple of cars, stopped at the next and ran a duster over the glinting chrome of the front grille. As he turned to move on, Gaunt caught a glimpse of his face for the first time and kept control with an effort. How Kriminalinspektor Dieter Mayr had got there, where the overalls and the rest had come from—the policeman plodding slowly up towards them as if he hadn't a thought or a care in the world.

Swallowing, he risked a quick sideways glance at Helga but her eyes were still on Vass with a hypnotised horror.

"Was Chiba next on your list?" he asked, trying to keep his voice steady.

Vass grunted. "Not till he was dead and I saw his picture and a story in a newspaper. I was over in Britain then, because I'd squeezed enough out of Gorman to know that MacIntosh and Ritter had been working there." His thin lips tightened. "I heard how Chiba had turned up in Yabanzan politics, able to buy his way in from the start. Then a contact I had in Yabanza came up with a story that Chiba had been planning a trip to Europe—and that when he was killed it was reckoned he was worth a small fortune, but hardly anything could be found of it."

Mayr was still working his way up the ramp, moving from exhibit to exhibit in the same leisurely style. Gaunt felt as much as he heard Helga start and draw breath, knew she'd caught on, and quickly tried to hold Vass's attention.

"But how did you locate MacIntosh?" He spread his hands in apparent puzzled admiration. "I mean, it couldn't just be luck—"

"I made my own luck," said Vass curtly. "If it matters, it took me a lot of time to find there had been a firm in Edinburgh run by a Scotsman, an Irishman, and a German—and by then MacIntosh and Ritter had both vanished."

He paused for a moment, frowning. The "maintenance man" had stopped on the ramp just before the car where Ritter and Woyka were standing and was bent down, apparently checking the tyres on another exhibit.

"But you still found MacIntosh," said Helga desperately. "How?"

"MacIntosh always liked playing about with cars and engines—in the old Commando, he was the only one who could keep our transport running. That saved our lives a few times, even if it killed him in the end." Vass grinned coldly at the thought. "I reckoned that even though he'd vanished from the building scene he might turn up in the garage trade, and I kept looking till I found him."

Down below, Mayr finished his tyre inspection and started off again, giving Woyka and Ritter a cheerful nod as he passed. The sight reassured Vass, but brought him back to what mattered.

"I've wasted enough time, Gaunt," he said softly. "I want that necklace, right now."

Out of the corner of his eye, Gaunt saw that Mayr had stopped again, just past the two men on the other side, and was running a cloth over the seats of a sports car. But whatever Mayr had in mind, he could tell Vass's patience had run out.

"It's in my pocket." He moved a hand in that direction.

"Slowly," said Vass suspiciously. He took a half-step closer, his gun-hand tensing and the stubby muzzle of the hidden automatic in his pocket suddenly poking its shape plainly against the cloth.

"Slowly," agreed Gaunt, sighed, and drew out the necklace. Letting the beaded strands rustle temptingly, he shook his head. "Ritter knows the inCwadi bead language. If you've the idea the necklace tells where Chiba hid his loot, surely Ritter—"

"Ritter wouldn't know what to look for," said Vass softly, his eyes fixed with an almost insane glitter on the beads. "I'll take it now—slowly, like before."

"Not yet." Gaunt moistened his lips, fighting for seconds, conscious that Mayr had almost finished his pretence of work at the sports car and, even more significant, that the woman had vanished from the entrance desk on the ground floor. If the policeman was going to make any kind of play, it had to be now. "What about afterwards?"

"You both stay here, stay quiet, and do nothing," rasped Vass. "Then later—"

A howl of warning from the other side of the car museum cut him short. Mayr, his phoney tool-kit thrown aside, had dropped into a sprawling crouch across the tail of the sports car with a revolver held two-handed, marksman style, training on Woyka. Two shots rang out like one and Woyka buckled back, dragging Hans Ritter down as he fell.

Sheer reflex action brought Peter Vass back to life after a heart-beat interval of frozen shock. He jerked towards Gaunt —then gave an animal-like cry of rage as Gaunt swung the witchdoctor necklace hard against his face like a miniature flail. The heavy beads tore the spectacles from his nose, smashing one lens in the process and momentarily blinding him.

A shot blasted wildly from the gun in Vass's pocket, the bullet whining like a banshee as it ricochetted from metal nearby. Still snarling, Vass started to drag the weapon clear but Gaunt grabbed him and forced him back against the ramp's safety rail.

They struggled there for a moment. Vass was the older man, but from that first instant Gaunt discovered he was up against an opponent with muscles like whipcord and a tenacity which had its roots in desperation. The man's sheer strength forced them back again from the rail and Gaunt felt an agonising stab of pain as Vass's knee caught him hard in the groin.

He tried an answering head-butt and Vass countered it. They swayed together, Vass still trying to bring his gun-hand round to bear, and Gaunt managed to hook a leg behind him, then throw his own weight forward.

They fell together, still locked and struggling, and rolled in a tangle down the sloping ramp to slam to a halt against the wheels of a motorcycle.

It shuddered and toppled, coming down hard on top of them—and as it did, Gaunt heard a strangely choking scream of agony come from Vass. Then the man's struggling became a wild, unrelated thrashing while the strange, gobbling cry sounded again. Suddenly, Vass was still and Gaunt at the same time became conscious of a red, sticky flow of blood that was soaking over them both.

Only when he pulled himself out from under Vass and the machine did the full horror of what had happened show itself. The motorcycle's handlebar had missed Vass's face—but the tip of the old-style handgrip lever had taken him full on the side of the throat, stabbing like a blunted dagger deep into the soft flesh, through tissue and artery alike.

The last sequence of Vass's struggle had been for life itself as he drowned in his own blood.

Sickened, Gaunt staggered over to the rail and clung there for a moment. Uniformed police were pounding up the rampway and others were on the escalator, heading for the top.

A hand fell on his shoulder and he turned, to meet Dieter Mayr's rough, ugly, for once oddly sympathetic face.

"*Danke*, Herr Gaunt," said Mayr in a gruff, almost apologetic voice. "I—well, I knew I could rely on you."

"It worked both ways," said Gaunt wearily. "How did you know where to come?"

"I had a location transmitter hidden in your car before dawn—and another in Fräulein Ritter's." Mayr shrugged at the rest. "We homed on the signal. But when we got here, I knew I couldn't risk bringing even one man in with me."

Gaunt nodded, straightened, used a sleeve to wipe some of the blood from his face, and looked around.

"The girl is with her brother," said Mayr as if reading his mind, and sighed a little. "There's an ambulance coming for him—he got in the way of a bullet Woyka meant for me. But he'll live, and Woyka is dead. I got in a clean shot, even if it was slower." Ambling away from the rail, he reached Vass and the toppled motorcycle. "You know, I can remember my father with a machine like this—the R32 model, two cylinders and five hundred cc's. They were good machines. . . ."

Gaunt left him and went slowly back up the ramp. He

passed Peter Vass's spectacles, smashed and crushed into the carpeting, and saw the witchdoctor necklace lying ahead.

Some of the wooden beads had been broken, trampled underfoot during the struggle. But most of the necklace was intact and he stooped to pick it up, then stopped, staring down.

A single, beautifully cut emerald glinted in the heart of one of the shattered beads. When he stirred the other broken fragments with a forefinger, a large, milky-white diamond rolled into sight.

Suddenly, cursing his own stupidity, Gaunt understood. Choosing one of the largest of the unbroken beads, he carefully placed it under his heel and brought his weight down on it. The wood cracked like a nutshell—and in the hollow centre, nestling in a wisp of cotton wool, lay another emerald.

Picking up the stones and the necklace, he considered them with a wry respect for the artist who had painfully fashioned those beads to such hairsbreadth accuracy, so that once the stones were sealed inside a mere patina of polish was enough to remove all trace of what had been done.

Whatever kind of politician Rionga Chiba might have been, his skill as a craftsman was beyond dispute. As was the cleverness of the way he'd chosen to smuggle his wealth to a safer place, away from his own turbulent country and an uncertain future.

Except that the result had been a trail of blood and death stretching over thousands of miles.

He drew a deep breath, shoved stones and necklace in his pocket, and started walking to where Helga Ritter was waiting.

Ash Wednesday saw Munich in a dull-eyed, penitent mood with even the clink of a bottle enough to make a strong man feel weak.

But the British Airways direct flight to Edinburgh, a sleek, white B.A.C. One-Eleven, took off exactly on schedule, climbed sharply above the snow-covered landscape until the city vanished beneath the clouds, then broke through into sunlight at its cruising height.

The aircraft was full and busy. In a seat near the port wing, Jonathan Gaunt sat with his eyes half-closed for most of the flight, a large single-malt whisky in front of him. His fellow-passengers thought he was dozing, and left him alone. There were plenty of others dozing on the aircraft, recovering from *Fasching* time.

But for Gaunt, it was a chance to think over all that had happened in the twenty-four hours that had just passed.

Hans Ritter was in a hospital room, recovering from the operation that had removed a bullet from his lung. Karl Strobel, already forgiven, was in the next room being watched over by Anna. Every newspaper, every radio station, every television channel in Bavaria was pouring out the first garbled details of a strange assassination attempt on a popular politician along with the news that Ritter was resigning immediately from any future career in that role.

Gaunt stirred and grinned a little. At least there was no mention of any outsiders involved and Dieter Mayr had also made sure that the credit for Ritter's rescue was vaguely assigned to an anonymous tip-off made to police headquarters.

Once the initial confusion and the inevitable statements had ended, Bill O'Brien had been among the first people to get to him—excited, triumphant, back in uniform, and with a couple of higher ranking U. S. Army officers in the background.

O'Brien had come straight to the point.

"We've got your fat friend Green nailed to a wall, Jonny boy," he'd declared happily. "The woman he was with last night—take away a red wig and that mask and you've got an alleged lady who was confidential stenographer to the military purchasing commission. Add that phoney clause he was trying to slip past us, and he'll never be able to sell as much as a lollipop anywhere we have a say."

Which meant the computer contract was being awarded to

Trellux. Patty might have gotten a new fur coat out of the deal, but for once that didn't hurt particularly.

Gaunt sat upright, took a long, satisfied sip from his drink, and looked along the rows of passengers ahead. Harry Green was sitting near the front of the aircraft, a subdued, scowling figure who had ignored him completely as they boarded at Munich.

Though Green wasn't particularly on his mind either. This time a quiet smile crossed Gaunt's raw-boned face and a stewardess, noticing as she passed, smiled to herself in turn, able to make her own guess.

He'd been waiting for Helga when she at last left the hospital, knowing that Hans Ritter was certain to recover . . . and if Rose Monday had been Munich's time for erupting celebration, *Fasching* Tuesday from then on until its midnight deadline had set an equal pace.

But for Gaunt and the raven-haired girl the hours had brought a total release from past tensions. A release with its own climax of fulfilment. What had happened had its own understanding and wasn't ended, though both of them knew better than to think too far ahead.

Gaunt was genuinely beginning to doze when the aircraft at last began its descent through more cloud towards Edinburgh airport. When they landed, it was raining outside and once through Customs and emigration, back among familiar Scottish accents, a lot of what happened suddenly seemed almost unreal.

Then the burly figure of Henry Falconer, in a raincoat and carrying an umbrella, brought him firmly down to earth. The senior administrative assistant to the Queen's and Lord Treasurer's Remembrancer strode to meet him with an unusually satisfied smile on his broad face.

"Good flight?" asked Falconer briskly.

"Reasonable," agreed Gaunt cautiously.

"That report you cabled yesterday left a few gaps, but we can fill them in later," declared Falconer, part of his attention on the other passengers emerging from the arrivals gate. "Ah —what's going to happen to the stones they found in that beadwork necklace?"

Gaunt shrugged. "They're going to be a headache for a few people, Henry. The theory is that Chiba was getting ready to bail out before real trouble blew up—so he chose Ritter to hold his nest egg, but didn't trust anyone enough to even hint what he was doing."

"A nice, juicy ownership squabble for the lawyers." Falconer nodded wisely, but still looked past him. "Let's just stay here a moment. There's something I want to see happen."

Puzzled, Gaunt glanced round and spotted Harry Green emerging from the arrivals gate. The fat man strode past them, sparing only the briefest of grunts in Gaunt's direction. Then, about fifty yards on, as he turned towards the car-park exit, two men in raincoats and carrying brief cases suddenly blocked his path.

"I told you I was going to find out a little more about our Mr. Green," said Falconer happily. "Stir a few Civil Service departments and it's amazing what you can turn up."

"Inland Revenue?" guessed Gaunt.

Falconer gave a satisfied nod. "A few small points about tax evasion. Mr. Green won't be driving around in a Rolls-Royce splashing anyone for quite some time—I guarantee it."

"Henry," said Gaunt softly. "You're a vindictive bloody-minded bureaucrat."

"That's right," murmured Falconer. "This is a good day all round. I—ah—took a chance and bought a load of those Trellux shares. Now, for some reason, they've suddenly started to rise. Did you—ah . . . ?"

Gaunt shook his head, watching the two men lead Green out. "Not with Trellux, not this time or any other time."

"Well, you know best," said Falconer awkwardly. "That leaves only one problem. You didn't get our twenty-five thousand pounds."

"Henry, he had a bullet in his lung," reminded Gaunt,

stooping to open his travel bag. "Anyway, I made an arrangement."

"What kind?" Falconer hopefully eyed the package in Gaunt's hands.

"I go back in a month," said Gaunt innocently. "And I brought this for you—if you like schnaps."

"One of my favourite drinks," said Falconer solemnly, taking the bottle. "A month from now—yes, why not?"

Something else had come out with the package, caught in the wrapping, a small, brightly coloured medallion.

"What's that?" asked Falconer, curious.

"A souvenir, Henry—just a souvenir." Gaunt tucked the *Fasching* medal away again and zipped up the bag.

Then he followed the senior administrative assistant out into the rain.